adrienne
maree brown

GRIEVERS

T0021895

BLACK DAWN  SERIES

"*Grievers* is a beautiful debut novella by adrienne maree brown, who is already one of our most important voices in Afrofuturism and true-life world-building. *Grievers* could not be more timely, tackling loss, plague, gentrification, memory and grief with a path toward hope in a future Detroit. Each paragraph is lovingly crafted, a story unto itself, blending into a tapestry no reader will soon forget." —Tananarive Due, American Book Award winner, author of *Ghost Summer: Stories*

"Dune finds her way into our inner spaces as we read *Grievers* by adrienne maree brown. We are compelled to witness this precise yet unwieldy unfolding spiral of memory and resistance via survival. *Grievers* is the right book for right now. adrienne inspires us to be present as we try and put ourselves back together no matter how broken this world seems. There has never been a love letter to Detroit and social justice lineages like this one." —Ayana A. H. Jamieson, PhD founder of Octavia E. Butler Legacy Network

"This Detroit thriller/mystery written by adrienne maree brown is a story full of suspense, grief and an overwhelming sense of community that is determined to survive a city wide mysterious pandemic. Each character will remind you of a Detroit Ancestor or loving comrade in the struggle and has you question what life will be like after hell." —Siwatu-Salama Ra, Community daughter, Mother, Detroit community organizer, prison abolitionist

"*Grievers* is a haunting melody. Highly imaginative but with a gruesome practicality, *Grievers* illustrates the lengths one person will go to in order to have some self-determination in the midst of being desperately alone. I was filled with the deep, aching love that was woven throughout this story. When all that you know and love is gone, gone up in flames, gone mute or just gone 'away'... you are forced to discover and draw upon all of the resources that are tucked into your family, your history, your city for resilience, self-sufficiency and the ability to truly make a way out of no way. Gritty and tender, it dug under my skin and settled into my Detroit soul." —Lottie Spady, Detroit activist and healer

With the Black Dawn series we honor anarchist traditions and follow the great Octavia E. Butler's legacy, Black Dawn seeks to explore themes that do not reinforce dependency on oppressive forces (the state, police, capitalism, elected officials) and will generally express the values of antiracism, feminism, anticolonialism, and anticapitalism. With its natural creation of alternate universes and world-building, speculative fiction acts as a perfect tool for imagining how to bring forth a just and free world. The stories published here center queerness, Blackness, antifascism, and celebrate voices previously disenfranchised, all who are essential in establishing a society in which no one is oppressed or exploited. Welcome, friends, to Black Dawn!

BLACK DAWN SERIES #1

SANINA L. CLARK, SERIES EDITOR

AK Press   AK Press
370 Ryan Ave. #100   33 Tower Street
Chico, CA 95973   Edinburgh, Scotland EH6 7BN
www.akpress.org   akuk.com

Cover art by Juan Carlos Barquet, www.jcbarquet.com
Cover design and logo by T. L. Simons, tlsimons.com
Printed in the USA.

This novella is dedicated to Detroit, and to the ancestors who inspired these characters.

GRIEVERS

Prologue

"We are beginning to understand that we have souls."
—*Grace Lee Boggs*[1]

Everything green bursts forth, breaking open any previous container—seed, body, concept, moment. Death is transition, it offers many faces, many sounds and smells, many distinct ways that a living thing can suddenly be absent from a body, which, stripped of the most obvious and appealing miracle, becomes a haven for any creature that can manage the stench.

Death is the way the old let go, leaving the young something to cleave to, to make new as they crawl out of the earth, becoming the home for the next life, unimaginable until it begins to breathe.

chapter one

Burn

Dune was new to touching death.

The body was heavy in a way it had never been in life; dancing in the kitchen to Marvin Gaye, holding Dune close to its breasts, thick and floating.

The body had a strange odor; ripe compost, late summer. In the last two weeks it had been impossible to keep the body clean as it died, impossible to acknowledge that the body was dying, even though the face was already frozen into a mask of grief.

Dune pulled it towards her now, her hands under the stiff arms, which she had never consciously touched when the body was alive. She found herself surprised at the cool absence of life, expecting warmth to be hiding still in those tight fatty places.

The body was resistant, as if tied to the bed. She pulled again and again, until the body finally came with her, dropping her down as all the weight kept its pact with gravity. The legs flopped open and Dune winced, the smell between the thighs sharp, familiar.

She rolled away, stood up, stepped backwards, some half-sacred instinct quieting her curses. She kicked the baseboard once and gathered her breath. Then she commenced dragging the body to the bedroom door, pulling alternately at the arms, or at the rug beneath.

Soon she was sweating everywhere and her back hurt. She noticed her physical discomfort from a distance, her self tiny and numb inside of her skin. This was so different from the weight she often lifted, trying to carve the softness from her body. When she reached the doorframe, she slumped against it, resting for a moment, the body leaning against her shins.

Sallow light whispered through dark oak blinds, leaving slat shadows on a hardwood floor cluttered with small rugs her mother had brought home from Morocco. Her father had splurged on the blinds in order to take naps. Now the bed's brass frame burned with sun. Dust motes, set wild by Dune's labor, caught in the beams, the only motion. The room looked quiet, peaceful.

Her mother would never have let the bed be a mess in daylight.

Her mother had kept a framed poster of Bob Marley in every bedroom since college and she'd put him over this bed after Dune's father died. No one else Dune knew framed $3 posters, but her mother, Kama, liked things to give the appearance of togetherness.

Her mother would never be in an unseemly pile of nightgown, cold greasy skin and soiled underwear at her daughter's feet.

Dune looked behind her. Down the hallway, through the kitchen, keeping out of sight of Mama Vivian, down the back porch stairs, through the tall grass, across the yard to the makeshift pyre.

She would do this. No one else would help her. She didn't want anyone else's help.

She would let her mother go.

....

Her flames were small in the spread-out city, black swirling up against the grandiose purple dusk that had swallowed the sky during her slow dragging.

Bonfires and barbecues were a part of Detroit's summer evenings—usually with cheap beer and a car sound system providing the music. There were less and less places to gather without needing to secure a permit or make a payment.

There were other kinds of fire.

Many nights, Kama had thrown Dune in the back of the car to chase smoke across Detroit's flat wide cityscape. Kama wanted Dune to know their Black city well enough to pinpoint the fire's neighborhood from across town. Closing in on a burning house, or abandoned warehouse, young Dune would be captivated by the way flames teased, licked up the outer edges and furled out of windows, always up. The sounds of the fires were oceanic, roiling and massive, crashing down floors. Sometimes brick would glow, but not give.

The fire department would spray water around the edges, letting the empty buildings become ash and air, trying to stop the damage from spreading any further. Neighbors would huddle on nearby porches, theorizing with Kama on arson and what the city would do with the plot of land, hoping it wouldn't be another skeleton of char or some flavorless condo; unclear what they hoped it would be. Kama's energy flowed outward, Dune's flowed inward, a perfect pair.

She watched the stars cross the night sky. Tonight, Dune's fire was no smoke signal, no cry for help or company, no crisis—she hoped her smoke would keep everyone far away. Tonight, her mother wasn't blazing across town. She was the fire.

. . . .

Dune had been sitting at the massive oak dining room table in the kitchen of the house she'd been born in, swiping through photos on her phone. She needed to find a new profile pic, one without Marta in it. Marta had been Dune's true love and then Marta had been a cheating bitch. It was time to break up on the internet.

Marta had taken this picture, her face soft, sun-kissed and smiling in the foreground. Dune angular, cool and dark-eyed in contrast. Dune was mentally berating her past self—she'd always known better than to put a "happy couple" shot as her profile pic, had given into Marta's sweet persuasion. Dune wasn't into social media, didn't trust it. But Marta felt the opposite, that things weren't real if they weren't documented, shared. She wanted everyone to know she "had a man."

Now none of the good solo pictures on Dune's phone showed her with her painfully tight cornrows, and she didn't feel like taking a new pic today.

Kama was washing the breakfast dishes, talking mostly to herself with moments of raised volume, which Dune felt compelled to respond to with grunts, amens. It was sticky hot, all the windows were open in gummy sills, fans twisting their necks in every doorway.

Mama Vivian, Dune's paternal grandmother, once a formidable Chinese activist in Detroit movements for racial and economic justice, was sitting on her throne in the living room just around the doorframe. Anyone who complimented the big old doors would learn from Kama that they were the "original wood," though Dune couldn't say which wood that was exactly and she doubted her mother could name it either.

The shadowy living room was the coolest place during the

summer, its windows blocked by the neighbor's house and the wilderness that grew between the two buildings. The air didn't move much, but it didn't boil either.

The configuration was familiar that morning. When Kama cooked or did dishes, Dune often sat like this, at the other end of the table, ignoring her mother companionably. Mama Vivian rarely entered the kitchen when Kama or Dune were in there.

The kitchen was a square room at the back of the house. It felt permanently crowded due to a monstrous table that Kama had gotten for free after someone else's divorce. They would never have been able to afford such a piece. It was a single slab of rosewood, meant for a dining room with a chandelier, in a suburb—not this railroad of tight spaces. As a family they'd sat around the table for meals a handful of times, mostly calendared holidays, squeezing into mismatched chairs that knocked against the edges of the room.

Their love for Kama showed in the swallowed complaints.

More often they took plates into the living room, eating on little golden trays that folded up and stacked in the corner. Other than Kama, the table was the only thing in their too-small house that was unapologetically big.

That morning Kama stood at the sink, her ass pressed against the upper edge of the chair behind her, head wrapped in cloth patterned with tangerines and palm trees. When Kama looked back to emphasize a point, Dune saw the sweat beading on her mother's brow and lip as her hands flew through the air with the sponge, the dishes and her opinions.

It was heavy in the heart of the room. Pots and pans hung an inch too low over the table from a silver grid, something Kama had seen in a movie once and said she thought was so elegant. Dune's father, Brendon, had loved doing things for Kama; quietly delivering her fantasies, even if he always did it a bit differently than the instructions. Kama had to have all the cooking options hanging up there: the wok, steamer, non-stick pans and a massive griddle that seemed to drag the ceiling down.

She only ever used the cast iron skillet that sat on the stove now, thick with oil.

The counter beside the stove was dominated by a decades-old wooden spinning smorgasbord of spices. Dune had read somewhere that spices lost their flavor with time, the bite and purity of flavor falling away. She'd started bringing home small bags of fresh spice mixes from the Spice Miser stand at the farmer's market: Chili Powder, Parsley and Rosemary, Lemon Pepper, Herbs de Provence. Kama would always say they looked "really interesting," and then put them up on a shelf with the rest of Dune's unused kitchen contributions, an impressive collection.

A well-worn bottle of Lawry's and a mason jar of nutritional yeast sat between the spice wheel and the oven. Those were Kama's kitchen moves beyond the obvious (salt, pepper, butter, brown sugar).

At the opposite end of the counter was the ancient maroon and cream rice cooker, used less and less as Mama Vivian lost interest in food and cooking. Brendon had used it daily; no matter what Kama was cooking it needed some rice.

On the other side of the oven was a little corner where nothing quite fit. Kama kept her broom and mop back there, even though it was a precarious thing pulling them out, banging the pans above into chorus.

Now Kama was saying something about going to pick up her check from "the capitalist pigs." "Of course they moved the office down to Fort Street, almost down to the bridge, because the truth is they *know* come winter it's gonna be that much harder to get over there on the bus. Its like eight blocks from the nearest stop. Naw, they don't even want us to get our checks that we *earned*. Like it's a handout! Half the city is on unemployment now! And they couldn't put it somewhere convenient?"

Dune couldn't fully tune in. They were living week-to-week on the tiny income she earned running dirty dishes to the kitchen at the Standard, supplemented by Vivian's social security and the tiny unemployment checks Kama had pulled in since getting fired from her last job for being "honest in the face of the bullshit."

Dune wanted to hear Kama say something about going to find a job, followed by maybe a couple of years of updates on how she was keeping that job. Instead, every day, her mother woke up with brilliant ideas for "making moves against white supremacy;" making lists of who she was going to call and mobilize. By noon she was caught up in researching conspiracy theories online, house maintenance or a visit with a neighbor to share survival technologies for some vague, pending apocalypse. In the evening she would go to or host meetings, always meetings.

Since she'd lost Brendon, Kama had become the child on the high dive who can't seem to jump. None of her ideas reached the point of having a fundraising plan, collaborators or anything that Dune could see as steps into reality. Dune felt for her—there was no place for the kind of grief Kama walked with. Her mother's complaints were righteous, but righteousness wasn't going to feed them.

The ranting rapids of Kama's words stopped some time before Dune noticed the quiet. Her mom was still standing at the sink, but now she was silent and totally still. Too still. The light coming in the kitchen window moved more than her mother, dappling Kama's edges.

The hair on the back of Dune's neck stood up. "What?"

Her mother didn't turn, didn't move, didn't sway. Just stood there, her back stiff, a wall between nations. Dune stood up and walked over, some deep quiet cell in her body telling her not to touch.

"Moms?"

....

"No, I don't think it's a heart attack, but something is wrong! I don't know what it is. She won't respond, she won't move. Fuck oh my god I think she just wet herself! Oh god—she's kind of crying, but otherwise she's really still! Like, frozen! No. No! No just frozen in place! Just please fucking send someone to help us. I'm sorry, but please!"

Dune stood next to her mother, yelling into her phone, waving her hands and trying to get a response. Mama Vivian stood in the living room doorway, fists pressed to her silent mouth.

When the ambulance finally came, Kama gave no resistance as the paramedics pulled her from behind the table, strapped her to a gurney, lifted her down the porch stairs and slid her in amongst the mysterious equipment they began attaching to her as the ambulance doors closed.

Dune rushed along behind the sirens in their little rusted brown Chevy, Mama Vivian in the passenger seat, chaste in her uniform of mismatched pajamas, a worn-down terrycloth robe, slippers and furrowed brow. The quiet ride through the overgrown fields and strange new buildings that characterized this part of Detroit felt eternal.

When Dune reached the emergency room she asked everyone where Kama was. The woman behind the counter responded in a flat voice, asking about insurance. The air caught in Dune's body. They didn't have insurance. Mama Vivian had something, Medicaid, but it wasn't much. Kama always said they would save money instead of spending it on something they might never need. Dune was pretty sure there wasn't much saved.

The woman was wearing a printed hospital top beneath a face that discouraged complex responses. Dune thought of how she and Mama Vivian must look, a panicking Black girl so boyish she was still being carded halfway through her twenties, with her confused Asian grandmother in house clothes. They weren't formidable, weren't used to wielding power with strangers; Kama did that. Dune began to beg, but the woman waved her off. "Honey, we'll treat her. It's just gonna cost you."

....

The doctors at Henry Ford couldn't find anything medically wrong with Kama. They initially concluded that she was in shock, possibly due to an allergic reaction.

Kama was a full-figured blue-black woman. She had been wronged early and often in life. She grabbed everything by the collar and pulled it in too close—love, babies, joy, pain, disaster. Her anger was as contagious as her laughter. Now her quiet was terrible and grand, filling up the small space behind the curtain and then the room she was moved into.

For four days they fed Kama through a tube, hydrating her intravenously as she stared at the wall. Her lips moved sometimes, but no sounds came out. A rotation of doctors asked Kama tons of questions that garnered no response. They plugged and poked and knocked her, snapped in front of her; always shaking their heads and making serious faces. They had conversations that Dune didn't want to be a part of, didn't want to hear; considering and then ruling out heat stroke, aneurysm, blood on the brain and a heart attack. They did scans of her mother's chest and head, ultrasounds of her belly, an MRI.

They were befuddled by her apparent health.

On the third day, Dune heard someone say the words "spontaneous brain death" in the hall outside the room. She walked out to calmly confront the speaker, kept her voice contained enough that if no one heard the words, they wouldn't know she was streaming obscenities. It was a kid, a nurse's aide. He apologized, red-faced, said that he'd been careless. He didn't take it back, his shoulders pulled in close as he sidestepped away.

Dune fumed for hours until the truth of it broke open in her own awareness. She could not move around the absence of her mother thinking, feeling, being.

A salt-and-peppered Black doctor named Rogers pulled Dune to the side and explained that Kama's brain activity was limited to the temporal lobe, the amygdala, and that no stimulation had generated any other responses. "She's not technically brain dead, it's more the kind of inactive prefrontal cortex we see in the severely depressed, but with the elevated stress hormonal flooding in the hippocampus that we associate with, well, with PTSD. As severe as her symptoms are, this does seem to be psychosomatic."

This meant nothing to Dune.

Rogers recommended a few weeks of observation, and shared what it would cost each day to keep Kama on life support now that she was stabilized. The number didn't strike Dune as possible in the real world. The hospital just needed proof that payment was possible, then they would transfer Kama to a long-term room. Dune knew she couldn't even cover the stay so far.

Kama would have to come home.

"But what do I do? How do I feed her?"

"Broth. Water. And keep talking to her. You never know, the brain is still quite mysterious." Dr. Rogers had a kind face, but closed. She spread her latex gloved hands, emphasizing how empty they were.

....

Two weeks later the city named the sickness Syndrome H-8. Dr. Rogers called and left Dune an urgent message. "We are sorry to bother you, but we believe your mother might be patient zero of Syndrome H-8. Please call me back, or when you get this please just bring her back down to the clinic."

Dune missed that call. She was busy cremating her mother in the yard.

chapter two

Gather

The morning after her mother was made into ash, Dune came to as the sun crested the horizon. She had passed the night on the couch in the living room, an alchemy of whiskey and weed helping her mind quiet for a couple of hours. The detritus was still on the coffee table.

The afternoon before, after sitting by the bed until her mama's skin was cold, Dune had wrapped Kama in the yellow flowered sheets of her deathbed and dragged her into the yard. She had piled wood, leaves, old print-outs of nonprofit strategic plans and other kindling under and around her mother, thrown matches into the chaotic pyre and blown her lungs out until everything was fire.

For hours in the moonless dark, Dune had fed the fire, keeping the flames rising. She'd been quiet as she tended the pyre, nauseous at times, a sense of burning up inside herself. A new feeling. An unbearable yawning emptiness. She knew that if she let it become a sound, this raging vacuous heat would undo her bones. Even when a longing to wail had possessed her small body, she kept it internal.

Now, in the hush of morning, she wondered if anyone had seen her, smelled her fire, heard her. Detroit nights were full of wild sounds.

The coming day was unfolding in bruised steel and lilac as she slipped out the back door and crossed the wild grasses of the yard to the fire pit. The sun reached its own small flames across the under-ridges of cloud. Dune crouched, sifting her long fingers through the ashes, still warm in places, unaware at first of what she was doing.

Kama had often spoken of being cremated into a seed pod for a tree or mushrooms, something that continued as earth, something that would grow.

Dune had read everything the internet could tell her about cremation. Four nights before Kama died, Dune ended up down a rabbit hole of pyre stories. She'd read some of the history aloud to her absent mother, partially for some accountability, mostly knowing her mother would appreciate the drama.

Burning was the best way to dispose of bodies that died mysteriously, according to a random comment on a pyre video. Commercial cremation left nothing behind, but outside of a furnace it was hard to get the fire hot enough to truly burn everything away. Cremation wasn't meant to happen in backyards, in the middle of cities. But Dune didn't trust the system, which had sent her mother home, to attend to this sacred work.

Dune had pulled concrete blocks and a square of stone into a kind of open-air oven. For the base of the pyre, she had used some wood her late father had purchased for a deck he'd never quite started. The sentimental wood had leaned against the side of the house for a decade, wrapped in tarps.

The fire had burned for more than six hours, her mother disappearing inside it.

Dune was grateful no one had come around, grateful their yard faced an empty building. Grateful now to have no witnesses as she dragged her hands through the soft pile, seeking.

When she found the first bone in the ashes, she gasped. This was what she'd been looking for. It was slightly rounded in her palm, just longer than her hand—maybe a rib. The bone was warm to the touch, dark, grainy, gray. She slid her thumb along it, rubbing her mother's ashes into her mother's bone, breathless at the intimacy of this holding, this touch. She placed the bone to her lips, and then between her teeth, pulling her shirt over her head. She wrapped the bone in soft black cotton.

Dune stood in the yard in her sports bra, boxers, socks and slippers. Her braids held, but she hadn't touched them since Kama got sick, so free hairs frizzed around her head, catching light. The cicadas were singing all around her, the constant sound of Detroit summers, pulsing, pulsing, singing of life.

She squatted down, brushing her fingers through the ashes with a greater sense of purpose. Each bone she found was distinct from the texture of wood, was smooth and sturdy in her palms. They had danced in the fire, not quite keeping their skeletal order. Here was one of her mother's long leg bones, these small bones were her mother's fingers, or perhaps bones from her mother's feet.

She found an intact section of Kama's jaw, her mother's skull.

Hours passed, the sun casting more and more light on the ash, sweat pooling at her elbows, behind her knees. When she couldn't find any more of her mother, she cradled the bones against her, swaddled in her shirt like an infant. She walked them inside, laying them on Kama's pillow, over the lace duvet woven with roses.

In the living room she found the two heavy "Chinese antique" vases Kama had bought at a street fair, pale pink, dotted with dragons, tall as her knee. She carried them, one by one, back out to the fire. She scooped handfuls of her mother's pyre ashes into them and although the remains were light, the vases and presence were heavy. She slowly scooted them back inside. Dune placed one vase on either side of Kama's bed. They were smudged with her mother, she left them that way.

Holding her hands up like a surgeon, Dune went to the kitchen sink and reluctantly rinsed with warm water. Here was the place. This spot, by the sink, was where her mother had been standing when the sickness came.

Dune looked out the window. What was Kama's last conscious sight?

Midsummer maples spread wide, clematis vines climbing aggressively up the black brick and balconies of the abandoned apartments across the alley, where the uniformly square windows used to reflect sunsets on good days. Now the glassless windows swallowed light. The stray dog that Dune felt deep affection for was laying against the far wall, tongue soft.

Mostly, all she saw was emptiness.

....

It was a morbid honor, being one of the first people to get sick.

Dune thought Kama might have been interested if it became a historical note, but then couldn't think of any pioneers of sickness.

The first people with a plague were never celebrated, even though that was such a frightening, innocent position, to die with so little context.

Hours after Dune had retrieved her mother from the yard, a police officer and an infectious disease specialist came to the door, two men, both wearing gloves and white masks over their mouths. They asked to speak to Kama, having heard from Dr. Natasha Rogers that she was the first person documented with these symptoms, which had now shown up in double digits. They expressed the requisite bare minimum sympathy when Dune said that Kama was dead, but didn't leave. In fact, their questions came faster.

She died yesterday morning.

Here, in her room.

The hospital wouldn't keep her, we couldn't afford it.

I haven't been on my phone...

She was talking, in the kitchen, and she stopped talking and froze.

Sure, right through there.

That was it. She didn't seem to sleep, she wet herself and... nothing.

She wouldn't eat. She wouldn't drink. She choked if I tried...

Her face just looked really sad.

No, I don't have a death certificate.

I cremated her.

This flummoxed the pair. There was some back and forth between them about whether what she had done was legal, Dune said nothing. The officer was pretty sure it wasn't legal, the specialist said it was smart. Both were unclear of what to do next. They advised her to do what she was already doing, staying home.

She only asked them one question, "Are the hospitals still turning people away?"

....

What had Kama been saying? Somehow loud, but also under her breath.

Dune sat in the kitchen after the men left, trying to remember. She had seen a movie where someone was able to see things in their memory that they hadn't registered in real time, but she couldn't remember if it was a documentary or something fantastical.

Kama had been pressed in here, between chair and sink. Dune had her father's flat hips, her ass didn't touch the chair behind her unless she worked at it. She missed the fat of Kama's body, missed the way life had pushed out of her mother in a million obstinate directions.

Dune turned to face the big table, to lean her weight on something, and there was Mama Vivian, in the doorway. Without words, her wide eyes and lifted brow said she was afraid, she didn't understand what had happened, was happening.

Why was Kama gone? Why had her granddaughter burned her daughter-in-law in the yard? What did the police want?

"They think Mama's sickness was the start of something," Dune projected in the voice she used with Mama Vivian, which worked sometimes if the hearing aids were on and the angle was right. "They don't know if it's OK that I cremated her here."

No answer. Her grandmother hadn't spoken a word since Dune's father died.

"We couldn't afford to have them do it." It would have cost three months of earnings to have Kama cremated through the hospital, not including an urn. "We don't have any money."

No answer.

"They weren't helping. No one was helping me."

Mama Vivian held questions on her face, but she wouldn't speak, dropping her eyes. How could Dune explain that she had loved her mother's body, and been scared of it—what can make a person stop living while they still breathe?

Was it contagious?

Were they next?

Did it hurt?

Who do you call to bury your dead when you have no money?

Mama Vivian looked up again, her mouth tightening into a deeper line, a slight nod. She wouldn't ask more of Dune, not even in her own wordless way.

chapter three

Holding Vivian

—

"Hello? Hello?"

Two days after Kama died, Bab came by.

For years, those who generally couldn't give themselves to any of the formal gods, but still needed to offer worship and devotion to someone had come to sit with Mama Vivian. They had faith, and when she'd had words, Vivian had had the best questions.

Vivian first came to Detroit in the 60s to support the work of the Black power movement, leaving her professor husband, Roger, at their small flat in San Francisco. Their marriage was a meeting of minds, it didn't matter so much where their bodies happened to be.

Vivian had spent her early Detroit days reading and studying, her nights going to various meetings with union leaders, community members, Detroiters who longed for something different. There was one particular worker, a brilliant Black up-south man with an Alabaman twist on every word out of his mouth. His name was Wesley, everyone called him Wes. Vivian loved working with him, and together they began pressing into some new intellectual territory.

For Vivian, it was the philosophies of Hegel that gave her a foundation to walk on. She saw what was happening, the crisis of joblessness, not as something at odds with economic abundance, but as a phase the city needed to self-transcend to achieve abundance.

Wes would respond, "Abundance comes through meaningful work, the opportunity to be somebody who means something to other somebodies."[2] Vivian found his vocabulary pedestrian, accessible; his concepts thrilling. They stayed in touch as she went home, comrades. She became a mother and a formidable translator.

When Roger died from an aneurysm a decade later, Vivian grieved quietly for a year and then sold the San Francisco apartment and brought her ten-year-old son Brendon to Detroit. By then, Wes was a handsome, divorced curmudgeon. He proposed to Vivian in his matter-of-fact way the first time they had dinner after she got to town, after insulting her musical taste, in the middle of a conversation about challenging the mayor. Whenever she told the story, she said she shrugged, grinned and said, "Why not?" They married the next day at a courthouse, united by respect and scholarship.

For thirty years Wes and Vivian had organized and thought and shaped the city, side by side. While he lived, she often looked to him for leadership, or thought of her work as supporting his. When he died after a short battle with cancer, she decided to continue moving his ideas for the rest of her life, humility keeping her from understanding that the ideas had been collaborative since he'd met her. Her love and grief grew their ideas into a beacon until people from far and wide turned to Detroit to learn ways to live beyond capitalism, beyond competition.

When she'd had words, she'd greeted students and visitors from her throne, an armchair draped in a nubby rainbow colorblock afghan, next to the window with its defunct air conditioner. Her kingdom was the yellow house over on Goethe, which she'd purchased with Wes, decorated with pieces of art that they'd brought back from their political travels together and, after his death, every photo of him she had.

After Brendon was killed, Mama Vivian went silent. People still came. They would show up unannounced to Kama's front door, having trekked for days to get to the city, the thinker Vivian Chin. Kama had set Vivian up in the cool cave of the living room, propped up by soft pillows never placed quite right. Vivian listened as her visitors shared whatever they needed to share—gratitude, critique, insecurity, longing, questions she could no longer answer.

Bab, an eccentric Black local, had been a weekly visitor for a decade, the only regular for the last couple years. She had gone to visit her daughter in Wisconsin for a few weeks and missed the start of the apocalypse. She was used to letting herself in, so Dune was caught off guard, having completely forgotten her. Now Bab birkenstocked into the kitchen with her standard mystery casserole—in tupperware, sealed in a massive ziploc. Her upward reaching curls and wide earnest eyes evoked elves or fairies. Her clothing was remarkably nondescript.

"There you are! You gotta get outside it is a *gorgeous d*— Darling?" Bab didn't know yet, it was in the tone of her voice.

Dune found she couldn't look up. "My mom died."

Bab collapsed into the nearest chair. Her mouth opened to say no, distraught. A tidal wave of questions poured out, flooding the kitchen, too loud. No one knew how to be tender anymore, it was all interrogation.

"I don't know. It's not clear. They think it might have been this syndrome?" Dune shook her head and sat down across the table, tired.

Bab shared her last memory of Kama, precious now—a random conversation that didn't fare well in the retelling. She said, "Kama was always so brave."

Dune thought this was incredibly stupid. The hierarchy of grief is measured in words and silence. The closer the death, the less words can hold it.

Unable to help herself, Bab came over and pressed Dune's face into her chest for an awkward hug. The woman was somehow skinny and pudgy at the same time, such that Dune could feel the chest plate between long soft breasts that hadn't known a bra in decades. Bab smelled like dandruff shampoo and fake lavender soap. Dune made herself tiny, but didn't push away, trying to keep some kindness together.

Finally, she said, "Thank you for coming. Mama Vivian needs you."

While Bab carried her inquisitive sorrow up the stairs to visit the elder, Dune escaped to the backyard. The dog was there again, as if he had been waiting for her. He sat close enough to be a comfort and she decided, officially, to call him Dog.

....

Dune could only handle a few moments of news at a time. Anchors spoke of the syndrome in the careless, drastic manner of the twenty-four-hour news cycle. In absence of facts, they offered fearful possibilities, theories, tweets from local politicians and performative condolences. Fox News had apparently shown video footage of "grief-stricken victims" the first few days, and that had led to massive backlash from families and local activists.

Dune was steeped in Kama's annual remembering of September 11, how she had seen and heard people falling from the buildings on her television, unable to look away or cover her ears. Her mother said it had taken her days to feel ashamed, to realize that her morbid curiosity had been someone else's terrified loved one, dying.

Dune felt differently. The disrespect was the death itself. The coverage could not make it worse, it was already the worst thing that had ever happened.

Turning off her radio, in the quiet of the house, she could still feel the panic of the city growing. Reporters and neighbors had come knocking, but she couldn't seem to move from the bed or the couch to open the door.

At night she would check the porch and find business cards, food, offerings of condolence—Bab must have let the community know about Kama. Kama's best friend, Elouise, left a note for Dune, offering to organize a memorial. Dune hadn't considered that and felt briefly feral in the selfishness of her grief. But she didn't move to pick up the phone and reach out to her auntie. Dune had always been the introvert who was pushed to connect with people through her parents. She remembered the memorial for her father. She didn't want that for her mother, a bunch of people in her face. She just wanted to lay here, undisturbed in her mother memories. Now there was no one to nudge her towards social behavior.

Another note was from a comrade asking how the sickness had advanced in Kama, because his daughter seemed to have it. Dune knew there was nothing she could say. It came, it didn't leave. They would learn.

The house was near Detroit Receiving Hospital, between two firehouses. Dune noticed the sirens of ambulances, fire trucks and police vehicles racing by the window with increasing regularity. There was a new signal blasting, but she wasn't sure what it was supposed to warn against.

H-8 was spreading faster than the story could be told. People who got sick around others were identified, counted, efforts were made to save them. Wealthy sick people were put on life support ventilators and tubes. There were people stopping in the middle of streets and causing accidents, freezing halfway up a flight of stairs, losing themselves while driving cars, which then crashed. Fires sparked as people got sick while cooking or smoking cigarettes.

One or two a day. Then five. Seven. Twenty a day.

How it was spreading from one body to another was not clear, or if it even moved body to body. The earliest notable pattern in the great Black city of the north was that only Black people appeared to be getting H-8.

In the quiet of the house, Dune wished that Mama Vivian would speak again. Not to bring an analysis to this moment, not with an answer to the mystery, but because Dune wanted to hear a familial voice, wanted the comfort that comes with sound. But her grandmother stayed silent, physically contained, watching Dune as the only point of information of the outside world.

And in the outside world, people of all backgrounds started flocking out of the city in chaotic migration.

....

Dune's closest neighbor, Gerald Thorn, managed the community center two blocks away. He and Brendon had been friends when Dune was younger, and Kama had cared for his plants when he took his family up north to their farm in the summers. His weathered, brown skin was covered in blue tattoos from another life, and his afrobeard reached down, gray and black in twisted tendrils that made him look as if he was eating an octopus.

Dune was tired of the misleading stories on the radio in Mama Vivian's room. She listened with hungry ears, never feeling fed. She knew that if she could make it to the porch, Gerald would pass by and give her some insight on the world around them, the sounds she was hearing. She stood on the corner of the porch, pulling on a spliff and wondering why everything looked so bright.

Dog came slinking around the house and leaned against the bottom of the porch, as close to her as he'd ever gotten. She felt like he was her wild friend, protecting her from passersby.

Before twenty minutes had passed, Gerald lumbered by. Dune noticed that he stayed at the gate, when he normally came in the yard and talked with one leg propped against the bottom stair, or while plucking a weed or two out of the grass.

"How goes it Dune?"

For the second time in her life, she said aloud, "My mom died." Her eyes felt sharp and sore for an instant, the tension between crying and containing nearly unbearable.

"I heard. Was sorry to hear it. Kama was... very special." Gerald kept his distance. She couldn't ask any questions, having said those words. Hearing her mother's name before the word "was" gave Dune pause.

Together they held the silence, Gerald looking down the street with no rush in his bones. Eventually he nodded a goodbye and moved along. Dune went inside and found some ham for Dog, feeding him over the railing.

That night the doorbell rang. When Dune opened the door

Gerald was halfway across the street, waving over his shoulder, "From Nina!" His wife. Before Dune sat a massive lasagna in an aluminum foil pan and a six pack of beer.

....

She found her way to the porch the next day, and the one after that. She wasn't sure what she wanted to know. After the third crossing of paths, Gerald offered his take on what was happening.

He stayed at the fence and Dune realized that it was proximity to her he was avoiding. He would never say this, but she respected it. She was one of the factors in the room when this syndrome began. She had touched and felt the first known body to succumb to H-8. She decided it was generous that he stopped by at all, a little longer each time, with more information than the constant media would tell her.

From Gerald she learned that ambulances were no longer delivering unclaimed sick people to emergency rooms, there were too many now. Gerald's son Jaret worked as an EMT, a lanky boy with a pretty face and a persistent nervous stutter. Gerald passed on that Jaret's unit's orders were to take the sick people who were found alone to the empty Technology Academy building off Second, sitting them one by one at the desks, creating comatose classrooms where nothing was learned in the murmuring quiet. There were volunteer efforts to bring broth and water to the school, as some people would still swallow. Volunteers with ill-fitting surgical masks managed adult diapers on these lost Detroiters. Very few people came to look for their lost loved ones amongst these quiet, grieving rooms.

It was from Gerald that Dune heard that several city council members had gotten sick. And that a perimeter had been created around the city, with the intention of keeping sick people from leaving, from spreading the virus. Gerald had driven up Jefferson to see for himself and came to the perimeter just before Grosse Point. When he said this, he looked as angry as she'd ever seen him. It didn't come out in his voice, he was a factual man, he was even keel. But his eyes hardened, he shook his head. And he looked at Dune and said, "I'm thinking anyone who isn't sick needs to be on their way soon."

The last time Dune caught Gerald, he and Nina were loading up their minivan. He said they had gotten a permit to leave town, only available to those who had had no instance of the syndrome in their homes. Dune wondered who was tracking that data and how. Every bureaucracy in the city was similarly chaotic on a good day. Gerald said they were heading for their farm up north where they often spent summer weekends, just until this thing blew over. Nina, a retired teacher, smiled over her shoulder at Dune, but didn't pause what she was doing—she was running the process of departure.

Even Gerald, this slow and steady man who always had time for a conversation, barely paused. He called out to Dune across the street as he lifted up into their van the things Nina rolled out to him. He said that Jaret's team was now estimating that ten percent of the city had been impacted by the Syndrome.

Dune didn't offer to help. She would not transgress their unnamed boundary and she would not make them speak it, to say aloud that she might be dead already, and they were not.

Jaret came out of their home with two suitcases as Gerald was sharing the news, his small 'fro wrapped tight under a bandana. He added, "Yeah, this shit is bananas. That storm yesterday? I went to unload at Tech and all the sickies by the window were drenched. They don't even move!"

Gerald caught Dune's eye and apologized with a shoulder, steering Jaret away. Dune waved at their backs and drifted back into the house. The next time she looked out Kama's bedroom window, the van was gone.

The next day she heard steps come and go on her porch without ringing the bell. She opened the door to find a notice folded into the screen.

9 PM CURFEW. EFFECTIVE IMMEDIATELY

Mayor de Costa has imposed a 9 PM curfew
for Metro Detroit.

All Residents:
Stay in your homes and within the city limits until the Syndrome H-8 situation is contained.

Food distribution shuttle schedules are up at
detroit.gov.

Dune scoffed and let the notice slip from her fingers back out onto the porch, closing the door. Home wasn't safer than anywhere else.

....

The house was sacred now.

Dune had never been oriented towards sacred things. She had the gift of a magical mother and had coasted on that, indulging secular interests, taking risks of spirit, knowing she was prayed over. She'd always known, without witnessing them, that rituals were being offered in her name daily, that her mother had surrounded Dune's life with protection.

Now every room Dune floated through was full of her mother's absence, the rightness of her mother, the things that could not be seen in Kama's living body, but beamed from her ghost. Kama's rage was more deserved, her rants more pure, her entire being so clear in retrospect.

This was the place Kama had crafted in order to become a wife to her husband. Dune loved their love story—Kama had fallen in love with Brendon the first time she saw him ask a question in a meeting. Before Brendon, Kama had never dated anyone who wasn't Black, or anyone shorter than her. But he was handsome, thorough, interested in the world around him. Losing his father so young had grown him up quickly.

Dune knew that Kama had grown up in an abusive household, her father beating her mother. Kama and her brothers had been brutalized when they tried to intervene, or find any aspect of themselves of which he didn't approve. When he wasn't hitting them, Kama's father was funny, sweet and well respected in the New Afrikan community. They had a tenuous relationship—teasing and funny when she was young and he could joke her into forgetting the most recent terror. And then colder and colder as she learned his weaknesses, mapped the dangers of his internal terrain...as she lost respect for him.

When Dune was a teenager, Kama had sat her down to talk about dating and sex. Kama had shared that her father had picked a man in the community who he wanted Kama to marry. And she had hated the man, found him boorish and regressive. And she had hated her father for trying to arrange her life, control her in this way.

And then she met Brendon.

Dune knew that her parents had secretly dated for half a year because Kama didn't want to bring the wrath of her father down on sweet Brendon's head. Dune didn't know that making out on the hood of Brendon's car out on Belle Isle had become making love in the back seat in the woods near the airport, where Dune was conceived. But she knew that Kama had become pregnant.

Kama's father never forgave her for getting pregnant out of wedlock, defying his matchmaking, having sex. He said she was a fast girl and couldn't be the daughter he'd raised. For her first years as a young mother, her father's judging rage had shaped her entire family against her, such that she had received nothing in the way of contact or support. She acted like she didn't care until the day she died.

She and Brendon had eloped and Kama had let her family slip away into their anger; had let her organizing community, Brendon and Dune become home.

This house was the place Kama had trusted to hold her child. When the time came, she had shared the house with her dead love's silent mother, who had never approved of Kama's protest-oriented politics.

Kama had been generous here.

In this house she had known abundance. Here, she had gathered all that she had in this disappointing world.

When Kama and Brendon bought the house it was a romantic notion. Kama had been round with child, this foreclosed and boarded up place had room to grow, even though it was in a seedy location, near the overnight homeless shelter. It was affordable with a few loans because the bottom had fallen out of the housing market. It was a fixer upper.

Neither of them were fixers by nature, so the things that had needed doing decades ago mostly still needed doing. The upstairs shower had a broken rolling door that had to be carefully balanced in both hands each time it was used. Three tiles on the kitchen counter were loose and no superglue would hold them in place for more than month. The pantry cabinet wouldn't close—there were rubber bands and nails to hold it, and they only worked during dry seasons. The windows needed to be covered in plastic each winter to create some semblance of fortified boundary between the snow and the hearth.

Kama came up with solutions for Brendon to attempt as needed and he was game for every attempt, but they were never long-term solutions. They were lovers, scholars, activists—the people were always calling.

While they rarely attended to the structural needs of the house, Kama loved to fill it with beauty. This African woman had surrounded herself with proof of her connection to a continent that had never been home in this lifetime.

Senegalese masks watched them from the walls. Cloth from her trips to Nigeria and Ghana were flung over every surface and pinned taut above windows to serve as curtains. Mountains of beads, necklaces and bracelets piled up and spilled over each table, handfuls of which Kama would grab and adorn herself with on her way out the door.

The furniture was thrift store finds, gifts, inheritances. To come into this house, an item needed a story. It could be a discount, a tragedy or an act of mastery, it just needed to be interesting. Kama found well-used things, Brendon allowed them.

Brendon hadn't much cared how the place looked. His weakness was books, newspapers, research. The touches of him around the house had been piles of books he was in the middle of reading next to his chair in the living room, stacks of newspapers on the back of each toilet, open history books and Detroit coffee table photography collections on the kitchen table.

Dune could still remember how Kama would flow behind Brendon, telling him to clean up. What she meant was, your stuff isn't beautiful. Only beautiful mess was allowed. His place in the house was the basement, where he'd had an office and organized his research about the city near the washer and dryer.

If they'd lived alone, the house would have been a hoarder fright. Being parents gave them some boundaries.

When Brendon died, Kama had slowly gathered his things from around the house, reluctantly, like he might come back and finish this book, or that paper.

Dune had found a cup of tea next to her parents' bed a month after her father was killed. It had grown into a mystical mold installation, so she'd washed it. When Kama noticed its absence, she'd screamed at Dune in anger for the first and only time in their lives.

Now, Dune understood.

She didn't want to toss the sponge Kama had been using at the sink. She didn't want to put away the sundress printed with women going to market, wares piled on their heads, the dress her mother had laid out to change into after breakfast the day she'd disappeared from herself. It waited on the bench at the end of the bed, as usual.

She was grateful Mama Vivian wasn't in a cleaning mood these days. The detritus of grief became Dune's comfort, the house her prayer ground. She believed in Kama. She lived somehow, being in the house, not wanting to leave it, or let anyone in, adrift in the life of her mother.

....

Dune was frozen. She was unclear if she was dreaming or awake, but she could feel, very clearly, the desire to move. She could hear it like a shout, the synapse shooting from her brain down through her motor neurons and down the thread of axon to her finger. To her toe. To her whole hand. Move. Move. But nothing in her body was responding. She could feel her effort, and she could feel the breathless pressure of drowning inside of her stillness.

She closed her eyes, willed a calming breath. Tears gathered at the precipice between her internal and external worlds. Dune realized that she had closed her eyes. She reopened them. The choice, that motion, unlocked her from the trap of her body. She gulped in a greedy breath and shook herself, shook her arms up over her body and out to the sides, flinging the freeze out of her fingertips. She tantrum-ed her legs against the bed, tingling in every atom, aliveness all over her.

Dune realized, in this unfreezing, that even if she didn't really have an idea of why she would continue living, she didn't want to die. She particularly didn't want to die from H-8.

....

Feeding Mama Vivian was getting harder. The old woman pursed her lips and turned her head away. When Dune spoke, begging her grandmother to eat, Mama Vivian would eventually take a bite or two. She only wanted drinks now: Ensure, milk, water. And strong Screwdrivers.

Dune started creeping out after dark to get what they needed, not wanting to run into anyone. She went to University Market on Warren, which had less people rolling the aisles each time. There hadn't been much in the way of grocery stores in the city for decades, it was a major point of contention and organizing. The stores that remained now had selections of picked over canned goods, boxed foods and the strange sweet stench of ripe produce and meat. She bought rice, beans, oatmeal, broth, stuff she could theoretically spoon into her grandmother's mouth.

Whatever had taken Kama was now a month old, sliding through the streets, swallowing people from their wakefulness. It was becoming normal to find people standing still in the middle of a sidewalk or street, grocery aisle or sitting in a running car, their faces contorted with some personal, mysterious agony. Their lips whispering random words, bodies rocking.

Dune wanted to care, but she found that she couldn't process the scale of loss. Her own load was heavy enough. She felt guilt for her myopia, but had no capacity to pretend to be interested in anything. She was trying to gather her mother now; every memory, angle, fact and story Kama had left.

And now Mama Vivian was trying to starve herself.

Dune's grief made her greedy for the silent woman's time, quieted in herself as she kept company with the thin line of Mama Vivian's closed mouth. Dune was holding on tight to her grandmother in all the ways she could. Offering unwanted sustenance. Speaking small jokes that could not be heard. Her entire life now was one continuous act of selfish care, but she felt justified. The old woman was now the last of her family.

chapter four

Model D

Dune was restless. This wasn't the same claustrophobic restlessness that had thrust her out of the house the day before. She'd gone out, fiercely stomping around the neighborhood until the late summer blossoms made her eyes water with repressed sneezes. She'd come home, dissatisfied.

Dune didn't want to see all the bright life outside. She had a toe tapping desire to run, but the territory was inside, inside the halls of her memory. She wanted to see faces, moments, to gather up memory with more abandon. She wanted to find more of her mother.

She felt how deep her loner nature ran within her. She'd had girlfriends, homies, weed friends, work friends, but she hadn't given herself over to the depth that resulted in best friendship, in the deep coevolution through friendship that Kama had with Elouise. Dune had mostly acquired people who wouldn't bother her with questions, wouldn't push too far past "fine" in a conversation.

Her coworkers at the Standard, and other restaurants before

that, were alright. They'd offered teasing comradery as she ran herself skinny from table to kitchen and back. But these were not friends she even had contact information for. And the lights at the Standard had been off at night each time she'd gone out this week, which made her notice that other restaurants were dark—was everything closed?

Her weed friends had stopped by the first few weeks, left her spliffs and eighths with homemade cards. They hadn't come again, hadn't kept knocking. It is the highest level of care, to keep knocking. She hadn't earned that from anyone yet … she hadn't offered it.

Now Dune wanted some kind of contact, but couldn't figure out what would touch her, satisfy her. Her life was too big for small talk, beyond petty drama. She had become heavy of heart, and hadn't built the kind of friendships that could carry the weight.

She agitated through the home, softly touching places that Kama had created. The altar in the front hallway, covered in incense ash. The collection of carved elephants under a framed broadsheet of the poem *The Elephant is Slow to Mate*, by D. H. Lawrence. The bowl full of stones with words of encouragement carved into them—*bliss, joy, love, inspiration*.

Dune had thought these woo-woo rocks were so corny. Now she pushed her hand into them and felt a memory of her mother coming, Kama stirring the stones, picking out an "energy" to carry with her throughout a day. She would often share it with Dune like a message from Jesus—who Kama referenced, called on, cursed and dismissed with equal fervor.

Dune picked a rock, just to see. *Curiosity*. The word was a bright furry green on a round rose quartz. She'd never seen this stone before. She placed her thumb on the y and it smudged. She wiped her thumb across the word and it came off completely. She shook her head, confused. "Cheap ass rock."

Curiosity was a luxurious energy. She couldn't afford it... There was little to discover that wouldn't ultimately hurt her.

She felt in herself a frustration with her mother, as if Kama herself had misread Dune with the erroneous stone. It came back to her now, the friction of being seen through her mother's exacting eyes. And then she felt angry with herself for remembering anything difficult about Kama.

She set the blank rock down and rubbed her shoulders, trying to push the energy off, or to contain herself.

....

She stepped into the kitchen, scanning for something specific, but unknown. The table was bare, the sink empty, the counters clean. The pots and pans hung dusty from the ceiling. The fridge groaned a bit, drawing her eyes towards it.

The light in the hall just beyond the fridge flickered. There, on the white wall that led from the kitchen out the back was the basement door, a towel stuffed along the bottom gap. The white paint had peeled off in strips, exposing the near-black of walnut underneath. Dune had helped that peeling along as a child, with her mother telling her to cut it out. In recent years, Kama had said she was planning to strip all that paint off and refinish the door.

Dune couldn't remember the last time she'd been down those stairs. Kama only went down there for laundry and, since returning home, Dune had shamelessly left laundry in the realm of her mother's work rather than fight for her right to do such a grown up thing. It was one of the ways Dune's budding masculinity had shown itself.

Since Kama died, Dune hadn't thought about laundry, had barely changed her clothing. Mama Vivian's soiled drawers were disposable.

Looking now it struck her: she'd forgotten to tell her father what had happened.

She felt hooked at the waist, jerked forward. Dune kicked aside the towel, grasped the knob and pulled the door open. Immediately, warm air gusted up into her face like a sigh.

Some mistake in the design of the house meant that there was a blower that pushed air into the basement instead of the living room. It never turned all the way off, even on the hottest days of summer. Most of the winter, Kama had propped open the door to the basement and set up a fan nearby to push the warm air through the house. "Just until it's fixed," of course.

In spite of the heavy heat, the dry breath of the house was a comfort today. Dune reached for the light switch and flipped it. Darkness persisted. She remembered then that the switch at the top of the stairs had stopped working last winter, and now only the one at the bottom would produce light.

She moved down into the dark, using her phone flashlight towards the end when the weak light from the kitchen ceased to be sufficient. She felt the space open before her, let her fingers drift over the wall until she found the working switch. Flipping it on, she stopped on the stair, paused by the parallel presence and absence of her father.

This space was him, cozy and spare; faint hints of mint, leather, prayer incense, sesame. She could hear him, trying to explain the world to her in his quirky, meticulous way. He was the dreamy

Aquarian to Kama's Aries, fundamentally unhurried, always trying to get a thorough perspective, even if that meant being in a near constant state of research.

Diligent and particular, Brendon had created a monument in the center of the basement, a large model construction of the city of Detroit, set up on four square card-playing tables.

To these tables her father had attached small wheels, so he could always move them around, reach the center. He'd tracked the constructions and demolitions of the city down here, the foreclosures, the opening and closing of businesses. She could see him now, sliding southwest Detroit towards him, slipping between sections to show her how he'd perfected the front of *El Barzon*, his favorite restaurant in Mexicantown. And here was the final resting place of Goodwells, the best vegan sandwich in Detroit. And by the old Michigan Citizen office, the Black-owned creperiê Le Petit Zinc, also closed. He'd put small black flags on each spot when its time was done, tasting the memories.

His eyes always looked sad, watching these changes across his model city. He'd said it was important to understand why the city was changing. "This is a valuable place. This is a valuable, fertile, hydrated, well-positioned borderland. Manmade displacement is never random, Dunny. Natural displacement? Sure, maybe. Hurricanes, tornadoes—even that, we don't really know, maybe there is a plan there too. But men always go towards something we want. Someone wants *this* corner. Who?"

Dune had been a young skeptic, not seeing why both of her parents were so obsessed with Detroit. Everything was falling apart, everyone was leaving—all she and her classmates talked about was where else they were going to go. She dreamed of living in a real city, a growing city. Detroit was not a destination.

Dune walked up to the model. It had been ignored for years, and those years had left the toy city dusty, the table wheels piled with the light fuzz of time, of not being moved.

There was a clear path to the laundry. Dune admired the tender discipline of her mother, coming into this place of her beloved, for years, not moving a thing.

Dune let herself get close to the model, the four tables covered in little plastic trees, patches of green felt for open space, small buildings gathered from board games, trinket stores, her own abandoned toy collections. It was always summer on the model.

Standing north of the city, the stairs behind her, she could look down Woodward all the way to the blue silk scarf that was, on this model, Detroit River, the city's southern border, a major barge thruway. She moved around in a circle, walking down the eastern edge of the model, beyond which Ohio was implied. Then she was standing in the river, Canada at her back in the one place where it was south of a US city. The tall GM/RenCen buildings were at her waist, the Greektown casino near her right hand. Opposite her, beyond the North End, waited the wooden stairs up to the open basement door and her mother's world.

This was her father's realm.

Brendon had done an amazing job of recreating the city. Downtown was built to scale, Dune recognized the massive L shape of Cobo Hall, the Westin a few inches north, the People Mover frozen on its useless circuit. There was a switch somewhere that was supposed to turn it on, but she couldn't remember if Brendon had ever gotten it to successfully chug its loop.

Her prescient father had argued on behalf of real public transportation. It had come, imperfectly, in the form of a light rail a couple of years after his death. It was supposed to expand to the west and east this year, actually reach neighborhoods beyond the gentrification zone. She wanted to tell him.

Though, maybe nothing would happen this year. Beyond the newest crisis of H-8 making her people sick, Detroit had been rationing water for some time—not for lack of water, but because of greed and mismanagement. Two years ago the city council had finally implemented a rightsizing plan, denying services beyond the downtown area, creating havoc and resistance north, south-west, east.

And beyond the city borders? The country was imploding along fault lines of race and fear. The norm was stolen elections, rampant corruption, bought and sold media, gutted and turbulent schools, and a never ending and unclassifiable world war.

A crumbling age. Maybe nothing would ever be built again.

Dune leaned closer. North of the defunct train, I-75 cut a path along the upper edge of the stadiums. Brendon had spoken of hooking up light and sound to the model and being able to rec-reate game nights, though Dune didn't get it. He'd always said it was the worst thing that happened in Detroit, getting swarmed by drunken white people from the suburbs who threw beer cans all over the downtown streets and stopped up traffic, honking in tones that were identical in victory or defeat.

Maybe, probably, games were cancelled due to the Syndrome. Dune hoped. A shadowy upside.

Just above 75 was an area Kama and Brendon used to take her often, to look at, to long for: Black Bottom. The stunning houses were mostly empty, boarded up or shelled out by arson, but Kama had told Dune stories of the elegant Black people who had lived out of those homes, where each family was a part of the city's

45

glamour. Kama had often spoke of growing up and having one of those homes, on the block where Joe Louis and Sugar Ray Robinson had been neighbors. Or the home where Delloreese Early was born years before she became Della Reese.

Brendon had glued multiple smaller house pieces together with curved lego attachments to approximate the unique structures they loved. His makeshift neighborhood signposts had the oldest known names of places on the bottom, moving up, each slip of paper a newer name, occasionally with gentrified hood brands in sardonic quotes. In the center was the largest sign, which said, Detroit (pop. 1,942,567). Under this was Fort Pontchartrain du Détroit, then *le détroit du lac Érié* and finally Anishnaabe/Kickapoo territories, Mound Builders.

Who were the Mound Builders? Dune didn't want an internet search response. She missed her father when she came across questions that would never be answered, not in his way. He told stories to say a word.

Above the highway, maybe a quarter up the model, was Mack, which became Martin Luther King Boulevard once it crossed the central meridian of Woodward heading west. It was no fancier for the formal name. The entirety of Mack/MLK was pockmarked with potholes that were refilled each spring, re-formed each winter, strewn with drug detritus and napping drunks.

Her father had done a particularly good job recreating Eastern Market, the largest open air farmer's market in the country, tinfoil and brick sheds with lots of small flowers and fruit piled underneath. Dune and Brendon had volunteered at the Grown In Detroit stand together every summer of her teenage years— Brendon interviewing every customer about their Detroit stories, Dune rolling her eyes and gathering cash.

Back across 75, two blocks west and six blocks north, stood the house she'd grown up in, the house she sat in now, nearly alone on its block. Gerald and Nina's bright purple house sat across the street with two languishing apartment complexes on opposing corners, fenced in, as if they had valuable things inside.

Dune touched the model house that her father had made into their home—it was just a little monopoly game house glued on top of a flat lego, but Brendon had brought her and Kama downstairs when he painted it. She could see him now, his face soft with pleasure as he gripped the little building in tweezers, dipping it into the actual sunbright yellow paint they'd used on the house's facade, and placing an X on top with a mangled paper clip. Detroit was his treasure map, home was his gold.

His placement was specific. Dune knew her parents had been proud of this house, of holding a radical enclave in the heart of the Cass Corridor. They had never adopted the "colonizer name" of Midtown that was cast over the neighborhood in the erasure trends of gentrification. Her parents had loved their outpost, even as they watched the heart of Detroit go pale outside their windows.

Now sunlight was shining on the model house. Dune looked around, trying to see if there was a hole in the wall or ceiling somewhere. There were no windows down here, but there was sunlight, a bright, active beam on the small house. Dune waved her hand over the house, but could not block this light.

For a brief moment, Dune saw Kama standing in the kitchen window, frozen, outlined in golden light. She looked around again for a light source and then berated herself inside, feeling foolish. She knew why she was down here.

"Father. Mom, Kama, is dead."

The silence hung around her. She wondered if she could feel him here, as the air, listening to her, or if it was just her own longing becoming a presence.

"She died of something they think is a virus, a syndrome. H-8. Maybe. She—we were in the kitchen. And she just stopped talking mid-sentence. She just ... went away. And never came back. She never came back."

Dune's voice was straining, her throat tightening. She needed to get this out. "She died here, upstairs. With me. I ... cremated her. In the backyard. So. She's here."

She felt the silence thicken, the stillness deepen, the basement go cool.

"Maybe she's with you? Maybe you already knew, maybe you're together? I just thought ... Are you?"

She held her breath, her eyes searching the air, the half-finished walls, the inanimate model, anything for a sign. Nothing. Nothing moved in the room.

"I hope you're together. I'm sorry ... "

Dune felt foolish. She didn't believe in this enough to make it happen. She pressed her hand to her chest, wishing she had the kind of faith that gave people visions, or second sight, or whatever it was called when you saw the light of your ancestors around you. Rumors, maybe grief-stricken lies, she understood that.

She just wanted, so much, for one more moment, to be a daughter.

On the wall was a shelf of supplies. Dune slipped around the northwest corner of the city. She thought of Kama, divining her rituals. Dune held her left hand, her heart hand, up before the shelf.

She was her father's child. She needed a something-to-do. She picked up the old jasmine tea tin full of pre-cut slivers of paper, the rubber cement, a pen and some paper clips. Her father had been prepared for every possible need.

Dune wrote "Kama Tutashinda Chin, birth date April 6, 1975" on a small sign, added her mother's death date on the back in tiny numbers, and fused it to a toothpick flagpole. She pressed it into the gray foam lawn of their model home.

She felt another chill when she stepped back from the model. She thought maybe haunting was just what ghosts did when everyone they loved was gone. Maybe no one would ever come to this basement after Dune. But if they did, if anyone ever unearthed this home and wanted to tell a story of the city, of humanity, of a family, they would know this was a living place.

chapter five

Dune's parents were strolling before her on the Detroit River Walk, no other humans around. The water was disturbed, crashing over itself, splashing up over the railing, onto the concrete. The sun cast a greenish tinge, and there wasn't a cloud in sight. No wind moved the air, but the river raged.

Dune called out to Kama and Brendon to wait for her. She tried to catch up to them, but they were walking too fast, faster than she could go. With all her effort, she was slowing down. She yelled out their names, but she couldn't get her voice loud enough. She yelled and yelled.

Her parents finally turned to look at her.

Brendon looked like he always had, except that his hair was bright white, as it had never had a chance to be in life. Kama's head was wrapped, as usual, her age hidden in her supple black skin. She had no mouth. Her eyes were big and she was shaking her head, holding up her hands up to make Dune stop.

The water crashed over the railing, a wave passing between her and her parents. When it cleared, they were gone.

She ran to where they had been, looked over the river railing, screaming without sound, trying to find them in the calming, tricky waves.

chapter six

Letting Go

Marta was on the porch steps.

Dune had been visiting her mother in the same way she visited her father, sitting in the bedroom so full of Kama's energy, half waiting, half longing. There was no way of knowing how long Marta'd been out there in the ninety-degree heat, Dune just happened to see her through the front window when she stood to leave Kama's room.

Dune moved too quickly to the front door, pausing only once her hand was on the doorknob, trying to remember what boundary she'd set with Marta. She couldn't remember the last thing she'd said, but she knew it was in anger. Maybe it didn't have to matter. Marta was here now.

Dune stepped out. Marta didn't turn around, but she shifted over on the stairs, making room. Marta was smoking a real cigarette, which she only did when they were fighting or her parents had had another violent argument.

Dune sat down. Marta blew smoke in the other direction, but

it doubled back and streamed over them. She looked over briefly, vulnerability shadowing her soft face.

When their eyes met, Marta leaned over and hugged Dune, awkwardly, sideways, hard. Soon, Dune felt Marta shaking with tears, breath hitching against her neck. Her face tightened into a mask as she put her arm around Marta's shoulders, holding her ex until the initial wave of emotion settled. Dune offered this grudging comfort with a small voice in the back of her head weighing in, *of course you have to hold her when it's your mother who's died.*

They adjusted in slight ways that reminded them of how well these bodies knew each other. They sat for a while, in the heat, Marta's arms around Dune's waist, like they still belonged to each other. Five years; they'd been together since they were teenagers.

Gladiolas bloomed in the yard, the warrior flower. The street was empty, heat rippling off the tar. There were fat, slow bees hovering, tasting; dragonfly pairs mating midair. Dune wondered if they were enemies now, carriers.

Eventually, Marta straightened against Dune and pulled away a bit. They contemplated each other.

Marta's face was lush in every way Dune's was spare—full lips, round eyes, childlike buttony nose, pillowy cheeks. Her hair was curly, brown, her skin golden, underlit with a blushed pink tone. Full heavy breasts, rolling belly, thick thighs bare under denim cutoffs.

Dune felt an absence of desire fill her up. She started the conversation to get it over with, knowing Marta could easily sit there for hours, quiet, seeping.

"What's up?" An impossible question, as good a place as any to begin.

"Why didn't you tell me?" Marta's unsteady voice was full of accusation. She sucked in her cigarette and exhaled hard, a fierce dragon.

"We ain't talking." Dune remembered now—Marta had asked for this boundary. Specifically, Marta had cheated and then wanted boundaries when Dune started asking questions.

"But...we're family."

Dune's memory and anger flashed forward like lightning inside her, bright and brand new. "We were. Then you fucked Max."

Marta's eyes snapped over to Dune's face, briefly, brimming again with tears.

"Kama was like a mom to me, Dune." Marta's voice was low, guttural.

True. Ish.

Marta had found Dune in the Detroit Summer youth organizing program, which Mama Vivian had cocreated with Wes and others decades ago. Dune's introversion meant she was perfectly happy with minimal contact, coming home after school to do her homework and then reading epic science fiction sagas, briefly interrupted by dinner. Kama had signed Dune up for the program to help her get better at making friends.

Dune was with DS from ages fourteen to eighteen, first gardening, then making community media projects. Marta joined the program the summer they were sixteen. By the end of the first week they were friends—Marta was also bookish, though much more extroverted and experienced at connecting with other humans. She would slip her body against Dune in hugs that woke Dune up into desire.

Early on, when they were friends, Kama often drove the girls across town to drop Marta off after the all-day workshops. One night, pulling up to the saggy-porched half duplex in Southwest, they'd witnessed Marta's parents having a front yard brawl, her mother held by the hair, punching her father in the belly. Instead of dropping her off, Kama kept driving, bringing Marta back for the night, no questions asked. Kama had let their home be a safe place for Marta to land.

"But she wasn't your mom."

That night the girls had talked for hours about Marta's family, and then what they each wanted out of life. Dune wanted to become a writer. Marta was a dancer who could sing ok. Somewhere in all the talking, Marta had leaned over and kissed Dune. They'd made out for hours on the couch in the living room while Kama was out running a meeting on the water shutoffs. Marta had practically lived with them since then, the young lovers acting like best friends, or sisters, but finding secret moments to slide fingers into each other, kissing for hours. Kama pretended not to notice, but when Dune came out to her mother a year later there was no surprise.

"You know what I mean." Marta was so hurt she couldn't look in Dune's direction. "It's been a month. You really couldn't pick up the phone and call me? Text me? Let me know, let me hear it from you?"

Dune remembered the way Kama had rolled her neck when she heard about Marta's cheating—*you deserve someone who is just thinking about you, baby*. Kama had been generous, but she was also loyal.

"I haven't been on my phone." Dune didn't even know where her phone was right now. She felt a pressure come into her chest, a breathlessness. "And ... I didn't know how to talk about it. I don't." With Marta it was better to just be honest, they were too connected for abstraction. But she couldn't talk about Kama. Not on the phone, not in person, not yet. Dune wished Marta knew that, knew to just shut up now and hold her.

"Dune. I don't know how to be with you ... but I love you. And I'm here. You should have called me. I shouldn't have heard about it from anyone but you."

"You broke my trust." Dune knew this to be true, but her anger was halfhearted. It all felt so far away from this moment. She had been sure Marta had broken her heart forever. Now that pain seemed so insignificant. Heartbreak for the living is still full of possibility. "It doesn't matter."

"It does too matter," Marta flicked ashes down the steps. "We're bigger than this..."

"We aren't anything." Dune couldn't listen to this round of arguments again. "I can't do this right now. I really can't."

"I didn't come here to fight with you. We have different values around this."

"No. It's not different values Marta. Lying isn't a values difference." Dune couldn't even yell. She felt like she was explaining something to a child. "You fucked up, it wasn't just 'oh our values were at odds on this one thing.'"

Marta was quiet for a long time. She had her face angled away, but her jaw was rock hard, her cheeks wet.

"Don't cry, Mar. Not over this." Dune felt an old resentment stirring her body, tightening her joints, making concrete of her face.

"I'm not! I'm trying not to! I'm so scared!" Marta turned then and looked at Dune full on, her voice climbing up and up. "What the fuck is happening here Dunny? We have to get out of here, we have to get out of Detroit!" She grabbed Dune's wrist, trying to change her. "My grandmother has room in Miami, my parents are leaving tomorrow. We could drive with them, or—I think if we take it slow my car could make it, caravan?"

Dune leaned back against the stair railing. Crickets were in full summer chorus. Whatever had killed her mother was spreading to others. Marta made sense, but it sounded like hell. Dune didn't know what to say.

"We?" She delayed.

"Yeah, we. You and me. I was confused! I fucked up, but I'm still your love. At least, I still love you." Marta paused and Dune offered nothing. "Whatever. This shit? We can fight about it when we are some place where people aren't becoming zombies all around us."

Dune blinked, saw Kama's stiff back outlined by sun rays against the kitchen window. She felt punched, and drew into herself.

"I'm sorry, I didn't mean it like that," Marta's words were too fast, desperate. Marta was always apologizing, never being more careful. Dune felt suddenly much older. She wondered what both of them would look like when they got sick. It wasn't attractive. "Dunny please. Please, let's go."

Dune wasn't considering it, but had never known how to say no to Marta. "What about Mama Vivian?"

Marta looked caught off guard. "Are you serious right now? That old woman don't even like you!"

"Fuck you talking about, Mar? That's my grandmother." Dune thought of the old woman, who loved her, trapped in her failing senses in the shadowed house behind them.

"What am I talking about?" Marta screwed her mouth up, looking genuinely confused. "Let's see... She's racist, she never thought Kama was worth your dad's attention, she hasn't said a word to y'all since he died. Come on, you told me that. Anyway, it's only Black people getting sick. We could put her in a home 'til it's over."

Dune's shoulders sagged, heavy. She was overwhelmingly tired. It would never even occur to Marta not to shit on Mama Vivian today, not to bring up these intimate and long ago disproved suspicions, shared with the tender confidence that lives in pillows. Even if Dune could stop thinking about Marta cheating there would still be this part of her. Dune had forgotten this selfish, callous part, the survivor instinct. Marta could never hear the no between the lines, always made Dune say it aloud.

"Mama Vivian is my only family now."

Dune saw Marta's eyes searching the ground, gathering a response, figuring out a next move. Dune wanted to stop her. "And besides, you and I are done." Left hook to the heart.

Suddenly Marta's nose was running a little bit, her eyes bright. "How can you be so mean to me right now?"

Dune shrugged. "Anyone you know die yet?"

"No." Then, again, the fumbling, "I mean yes, obviously, Kama of course. It's, they're all over the city, Dune. They are talking about a quarantine. We can't stay here, Dunny. It's ... it's devastating."

Dune felt the arguments piling up inside her. No, devastating is losing your mom in an instant. Devastating is burning your mother in the yard. Devastating is becoming an orphan before turning twenty-five. Devastating might even be finding out the person you love is a liar. But, then, Dune also knew devastating is watching your hometown go ghost.

"I'm not leaving. But you should. We don't know what this is. Or how it works. You should go."

"So you at least care whether I live or die." Marta turned away again. Dune knew all of these moves by heart. Marta spoke quietly,

"I can't believe you fell out of love with me. I can feel it. I can see it in the way you look at me... Oh god it really hurts."

The quiet grew. Dune could feel the unspoken words she was supposed to say in this moment sliding up between them, a glass partition. It hurt her too. But she didn't want this anymore. There were so many small reasons under the big one.

"My mom just died Mar." Dune felt the pressure move from her chest up into her throat with this fourth articulation of her impossible new reality. It took such effort to speak. "I didn't fall out of love with you. You broke the part of me that was able to love you. And now I see you as you are—you're not a bad person, Mar. But you're not an honest person, either. Something like this doesn't just happen—"

"But—" Marta was turning again. Dune kept hearing the word goodbye in her head.

"It doesn't, babe. But even if you hadn't cheated, I don't have shit to give you right now. There's nothing." Dune gestured loosely at her chest, the landscape that had once been so green for Marta. She felt a dry husk inside her. As she said it, she felt the truth of it, the absence of any real feeling.

She wanted to make sure Mama Vivian was ok, give her some water.

She wanted to take care of her parents' home.

She wanted to go back inside and crawl in bed with her mother's bones.

They were quiet for a while. Dune turned to face the street. Some impulse made her slip an arm around Marta, generous with the end in sight. Marta quickly leaned onto Dune's shoulder. They sat that way for a quiet length, too hot, Marta emoting some more in little hitches, pooling a Rorschach onto Dune's shirt.

After a while Marta sat up, flicking tears from her face like she did ash from her cigarette. She smoothed her hair back and stood up, facing Dune, stamping out her smoke. She looked empty, deflated, clear.

Marta leaned in, took Dune's face in her hands, and kissed her, gentle, slow and innocent, once on the mouth, and once on the forehead. Her hands lingered for a moment before dropping.

"Ok," she said, clearing her throat. "See you."

Dune nodded, the pressure now in her shoulders, jaw, tongue. She didn't think they would see each other again.

Marta turned and walked to the street. She paused at the small gate for a moment and looked back. Dune wondered what Lot's wife's name was. She saw Marta in that moment as if looking through a warp in time, the sun a brighter color, in a city where death could be avoided. She saw, briefly, her love, her tender sweet love.

But then Marta was walking, her beautiful sashay reduced to a shuffle that let Dune know she was crying as she left. If she'd had the right attire on, Marta would be ripping at her clothes and wailing; she felt everything at the level of her skin.

Dune knew this wasn't really even a choice, all she could do was observe the truth; this tiny love couldn't fill her palm, couldn't even be seen in the cave of her heart. She sat on the porch and let herself soften, wishing for a breeze, a respite. She noticed that it was beautiful outside, the heat, the heavy brightness, the verdant span of life bursting, bushes drooping with thick flower, sidewalks splitting with new growth at every seam. It had been a fucking beautiful summer.

When Marta was gone, Dune pressed her palms against her eyes, resting her elbows against her knees, and rocked herself.

....

Dune was making love to Marta.

They were in the backyard, next to the fire pit. Marta was on top of her, hair in pony tails like when they first met, no panties under her skirt, her white sweater pulled up, nipples gathered into hard knots at the tips of smooth creamy breasts, heavy over her soft belly. Dune was sucking sweet warm milk first from one breast, then the other, while Marta rocked down against her.

From the side of her eye, Dune noticed that Marta was fading, one part at a time, left hand, then arm, right arm, legs below the knees. All the while she kept speeding up, thrusting herself bare against Dune's pelvis.

Dune reached up and held Marta's hips, tried to reach her fingers down and into her lover, to keep her here. As soon as she touched the wet, it was gone. Marta's neck faded, her jaw, but Dune kept drinking from her, even when Marta was just weight, eyes, pleasure mouth, nipples. With an orgasmic gasp and shudder, Marta was gone, leaving a sticky mess all over Dune's belly, crotch and thighs.

Dune realized the fire pit beside her was raging, strange faces watching her from the flames, filling the whole sky with smoke.

chapter seven

Strange Patterns

There was an envelope in the screen door.

It was thick, white, bent by the door's pressure, no words on the outside, but some stuff crossed out from previous use. It was taped along the seal, which she appreciated—she always cringed at the idea of touching other peoples' dried spit.

She looked across the street and around, but no one was in sight.

Dune backed into the house, sat on the stairs and tore open the note. Inside was a wad of money wrapped with a piece of paper and secured with a rubber band. She pulled the paper open.

This message is for Dune Chin and any other surviving relatives of Brendon Chin.

Dune felt her breath catch and crushed the letter between her hands for a moment, closing her eyes against the memory of her father in the hospital, somehow both swollen and crushed, bruised and bloodied, gone and there, the three women of his life touching him as he left his body.

She exhaled and flattened the paper against her thighs, the exploring energy of the morning deflated as she picked it up again.

I saw your mother's name on the list of those whose lives have been claimed by H-8. I have never forgiven myself for taking your father from you. I have not driven a bus since that day. A lot in my life has changed. Many times I wanted to come visit you. Your mother said I could. She said that she had done the work to forgive me. But I couldn't face you, her or Mrs. Chin.

I sent your mother some money over the years. Not enough. The settlement never felt like enough. I know nothing ever could.

I am leaving Detroit now. Maybe you are gone already, but it looks like you are there. Here is everything I can spare. Please get to safety.

With eternal sorrow,
Paulie Vereen

Dune looked at the money. It was hundred dollar bills, Ben Franklin's stern face over and over. She counted the bills till she got to thirty, still she wasn't a tenth of the way through the stack.

This would have been a godsend two months ago, when it could have covered Kama's hospital care, extended her life. Dune felt her system try to catch the spark of grief or anger, but she was thumbing an empty lighter. She took the money to the altar in Kama's room. She placed the envelope under the picture of Brendon that was the center of the sacred space.

Then she fell into the bed, praying to dream of her parents.

....

The next morning, after taking care of Mama Vivian, Dune was cleaning dishes when she felt the pull to visit the basement again.

Each day since adding Kama to the model, she had gone down and added other names that she found printed in the papers. She hadn't decided to do this, had simply found herself drifting over and over towards the basement darkness. Once down there, she opened the Citizen on her phone and found the names, addresses.

This morning she flipped on the basement light and saw right away that something was different on the model. She stepped closer. A strange green mold was growing on the foam. Right around their little gold monopoly house.

It made her sad—she didn't want any signs of decay down here. She grabbed a napkin from Brendon's supplies and wiped the mold away.

The next day it was back, a persistent little algae on the ground around the house and a little bit at the base of the toy building. She told herself basements are damp, it made sense there would be mold. It was a small problem. She had big ones to attend to.

chapter eight

Food

Autumn came in shocks, the temperature dropping as if slipping down a stair, recovering itself into some balance, and then slipping again on the next step. It had been such a sticky summer, and the heat didn't seem ready to release the city, sliding back in after each cold snap, a lover returning for one more kiss.

This was usually Dune's favorite season, all the sunlight that had poured into the city through the summer months would soon show out as the treetops went to blaze, ginkgo lighting up into sun-bright golden spheres, burnt red spreading across maple and pear leaves in fractal fires; the rainbow of leaves covering cars and yards.

It was the best season to bike or drive on the roads of Detroit. In the winter there was sleet and soiled snow in car catching piles, hidden potholes. In the spring the city sent teams out to fill the holes, but they moved at the pace of bureaucracy and the roads were still treacherous. In the summer the holes were filled, but these days it got so hot that the road seemed to ripple underneath each wheel. Finally, fall arrived. It was cool enough to be outside and the roads were as smooth as they would ever be. And the perilous children, who biked in zigzags and darted into the street for bouncy balls, they were all in school.

This year everything was different. Detroit Public Schools had announced that they were delaying the start of the school year until further information emerged about H-8. The curfew was being upheld by a police force that was equal parts timid and reactionary. People were trying to go about business as usual and Dune learned what persisted in the face of death—stores kept up shorter hours, barbers and hairdressers offered "H-8 Discount Rates," a lot of higher end restaurants closed, but the Coneys were still there, selling chili cheese fries and hot dogs at all hours of day and night. The weed dispensaries sent promotional texts with "syndrome specials."

Dune noticed how life went on. The postal service continued and she wondered who these brave people were, moving from house to house, not knowing what was behind the doors or how H-8 spread. Food delivery boomed as those who could afford it tucked into their homes and let the poor take the risk of outdoors. There were still humans driving ambulances, with other humans in the back hopping out and loading up the freshly absent and those who died in other ways, because that still happened. Even with the option of H-8, some bodies still chose to try other methods of escape—heart attacks, heat stroke, deep vein thrombosis, pneumonia, choking, shot by police, overdose.

Dune also noticed the ways in which Detroit was obstinately itself. No one stopped at red lights, just slowed down and rolled on through. This was usual at night, but now as the city shrank, she saw it happen more and more often in broad daylight from the porch. Who had life to waste waiting at these uncontested lights?

The Daily Crime Report indicated that forty-two people had been shot over the summer. Reports of break-ins were increasing, according to Metro Protective, the biggest security company. They initially requested that those evacuating the city not leave their alarm systems on, but everyone did and soon the systems were overrun as those left behind started scavenging. The company then announced that they would not respond to notifications if no one answered the verification call to the landline.

Everyone who stayed was balancing risk aversion and self-delusion, as if there was still any safety left.

A developer from DC arrived in August saying he had figured out a solution to H-8. He was given a front-page story in the *Detroit News*, above the fold. The photo of the white man—dark hair combed back in a smooth wave, suit crisp—felt familiar. Dune wondered if there was a factory somewhere that just produced white men who could see the future of Detroit, a place where she could go and toss a wrench in the gears. She was not surprised that he knew nothing and slipped away from the public eye when it became clear that the only abundance he could tap into was panic. Dune was frightened, annoyed and amused, like everyone else.

Fall came to Dune from two places—the trees flecked with fire's palette outside Kama's window, and the news on her phone and Mama Vivian's radio. Summer was gone and H-8 had had a voracious opening season.

....

Dune wondered where she could find out who was here and who had gone, even just amongst the people she knew. What were the numbers of the city now, in this rapid tragedy?

She couldn't look at social media—her notifications were full of people sending "prayers and love" to her, or her family, or to the city of Detroit. At some point, these trite condolences had replaced the act of grieving, of actually feeling a wave of sadness. Before, a loss could make you gasp. Before, it reached your heart. You were expected to have a coherent articulation for it, a way to say you knew something had happened and you had the right response. These meaningless words, combined with conspiracy theories, misguided cancellations and misinformation, made it too nauseating to even log on.

She let Mama Vivian's radio be her main source of information, even though it wasn't necessarily more accurate. She was putting the names of the deceased on the model now, names she sometimes recognized or felt she should have known. Hundreds of names.

The main theory running the news cycle now was that tap water was somehow to blame for this sickness. Dune thought it was an informed suspicion, given the battles against lead-poisoned water up the road in Flint and the years of tension over water control in Detroit. Kama had had her hands buried in sink water when she'd gotten sick. It was a theory, but Dune felt more practical than conspiratorial. She was beginning to feel aware of her own aliveness again—not quite a desire to live, just a growing, surprising awareness that she was not dead. Sometimes, while longing for her mother, she wished she could cross over. But still, she was not dead. She felt, however slight, the pull of life.

....

Dune had always suspected that Mama Vivian was selective with her deafness. Not necessarily by choice—it was more like her ears wouldn't let in any small talk.

Dune still came to sit with her, to be company. Once, she started humming. The humming gave way to Otis Redding.

Sittin' in the mornin' sun
I'll be sittin' when the evenin' comes
Watchin' the ships roll in
Then I watch 'em roll away again

She was humming and singing with her eyes closed, but when she peeked, Mama Vivian's eyes were on her, mouth open in a near smile. Dune slipped into another song, a slow one she'd written.

My heart is a song
With lost words
I don't know the way
To the end
What else can I do
But pray up
My song is a wave
Crashing shore

Mama Vivian's attention indicated that she liked this one, especially when Dune let her voice open and fill the house up for the last little verse. Dune sang then, gospel hymns with gaps in the words, Sam Cooke, Ella Fitzgerald, until Vivian fell asleep.

....

The gate on the chain-link fence guarding the community garden on Brainard was sagging open, detached, done.

Dune almost passed it by without stopping, but her eyes darted in, parsing amongst the overgrowth. She first recognized small green watermelons fat on the vine, then speckled pears fallen from a tree heavy with the brown fruit. She slowed, checking the street for owners or witnesses. Seeing none, she slipped inside.

Kama and Brendon's voices entered the front room of her memory, arguing over this garden. Brendon made the case that, "good fences make bad community gardens." Kama countered, "I fully get the desire to protect the wealth in the soil." Although, her strategy was more gardens, not more fences.

The week before, Dune had biked over to stand in line for a grocery bag of free food and bottled water at the emergency center at Woodward and Grand. She couldn't sort out within herself if she did this for Mama Vivian, for herself, or simply to have something to do. Like most free food, the bag of cans and boxes was underwhelming.

Whole Foods had closed its doors once those with money fled the spreading sickness, evacuating their workers in what was viewed as unexpected benevolence. Dune's vague interest in boutique international cuisine had faded accordingly. She went to University Market to get non-perishables. It was one of the few shops bigger than a party store that was still consistently open in the city limits, though the shelves were getting light as less vendors were willing to resupply within city limits. The only meat options they had were frozen piles of ground beef, fish, thousands of drumsticks and chicken breasts to thaw. Even the Detroit Community Co-op closed their doors after three volunteers had gotten sick on the same day.

They said temporarily. Everyone did.

Time was losing meaning. Food was reduced to fuel; Dune was primarily concerned with what would give her and Mama Vivian nutrients. Right now, they needed vegetables, not the processed stuff left on the shelves, stacked in the donation bags.

This garden was definitely picked over, footprints and haphazard vegetables here and there, as if people had rooted through it looking for something else. Still, there were perfectly fine cucumbers and tomatoes left on the vine and a lot of things she didn't quite recognize that looked like lettuce or collard greens.

She grabbed all the food she could load into her bike's saddle baskets. She was trying to balance a massive squash on top when two men walked around the corner, laughing with each other. They were unhurried, at ease with each other. Black men in Detroit gave off a sense of being unflappable, adapting to the changing conditions with a shrug and a swagger. When these two saw her, they paused and she froze. She wasn't sure if she was stealing.

"What's good?" she said, tentatively.

The taller of the men laughed out loud. The other one shook his head saying, "Don't trip. This ain't our shit."

The tall one, still laughing, said, "I mean it's all our shit now. Losers weepers."

She nodded, waved an odd salute at them and pushed off. She kept turning her head to the side just enough to see them in her periphery, half wishing they were her boys, that she could move with men like that. Soon they were inside the garden fence, loading up their arms.

Etta James took the stage in Dune's head, singing about a man as an object that could be lost, found, mistreated, cherished, wept over.

I been in love with your man for a long, long time
Yes I have, you didn't know that did you?

I been trying to think of a way to make him mine
Now listen, I will still be your best friend and do all, do all I can
Sure enough, but I'll never, never, never let go of that man
Because it was a case of
Losers, weepers, finders, keepers

In Detroit though, the losers didn't weep. They panicked, they evacuated. The lost? They became both object and weeper.

She wheeled her bike around to the back of her house, unloading her small harvest. She put away things she recognized, leaving piles of green leafy mystery on the table to research.

In spite of Kama's best efforts, Dune had never been a particularly healthy eater of her own volition. She was a graduate of DPS, meaning she'd grown up eating chicken nuggets, pale sweetened vegetables, and pizza on Fridays.

Marta had sometimes been a good influence during their years together, had talked Dune into only eating raw foods for a month, juicing, making a salad be a whole meal. Luckily Marta was as inconsistent in food as she was in love, so they still got to have hot cheetos and brownies when they were high.

It had been a month since Dune had seen Marta. She wondered if Marta had made it to Miami, if she was staying with her parents, if she was living a normal life, if she was… Dune caught herself. She couldn't keep giving any seeds of attention or longing to Marta's infertile soil.

Dune stopped by Kama's table and right on top of the bowl of stones was a jagged purple rock that said *Nourish*. Dune smiled, feeling like her mother was proud of her. Then she wiped the rock as a test and, once again, the letters came off in a thin green film that stained her thumb. "What the fuck?" She looked around, feeling a little disconcerted, a little dumb, a little played by what appeared to be ancestral jokes.

She carried some of the mystery greens upstairs and showed them to Mama Vivian, who cocked an eyebrow at her and then returned to looking out the window. Dune wondered, not for the first time, if her grandmother was just deeply unimpressed by her. She was the shy daughter and granddaughter of adults who had filled up all available space with words, analysis, cutting each other off to get their points across. It had been easy for Dune to take on a listener shape in her family. But now it was hard not to take the silence personally.

The old woman had given up speaking, she no longer needed a listener. And Dune didn't know how to fill space. Most of the time it felt like she had too much happening in her head to get it coherent in her mouth.

Carrying the mysterious vegetables back down the stairs, Dune decided to ride around and check out the other community gardens nearby, reconnaissance to clear her head.

The gardens she knew of were at 2nd and Willis, down John R and a big one on Warren, in the southernmost corner of Wayne State. The Wayne State Garden had security and looked as it were being well tended. The other two were ripe with unpicked food.

She was not alone as she entered these, there were others with baskets, plastic bags, cardboard crates. A trio was gathering greens methodically in the corner, their faces covered. They didn't look up.

Dune started in the other corner where no one was working. She didn't feel guilty for entering these gardens and no one looked askance at her as she began to part the greens and try to figure out what was in the dirt. The abundance of the gardens amazed Dune and she couldn't figure out how anyone ever learned to know what they were looking at. She could tell broccoli from eggplant, but just barely.

There were nods, grunts of hello, and she overheard the low murmur of news being exchanged. Everything was done at a distance, each person or group setting their own cone of safety about them, holding it without words.

Dune had been with Kama when she got sick and as she died. She wasn't much worried about proximity to H-8, but she appreciated that the boundaries indulged her persistent need for solitude. There were no interactions in these gardens that she needed to fret over or reject. She could feel the ghosts of her parents at her back, how they would have called out hello, reached out with questions and theories, started to think of ways to organize resources together with others who were staying. Dune shrugged them off of her, focusing on finding food she wanted.

She didn't know what was a good find. She avoided obvious problems, splits or bruises in the skin. Some of the greens had small brown bugs tucked in amongst the leaves or dotted white creatures, but that seemed normal? She had the best luck with things that were still underground, which she pulled up primarily to find out what they were. She discovered carrots, turnips, onions, beets, kale. And then more cucumbers, cabbage and some tiny tomatoes wrapped in a soft wrinkled brown skin that popped sweet in her mouth. She held one up to the light and a fellow forager called out, "Those are ground cherries. Makes a good jam!" Dune raked up several handfuls from the dirt.

At the end of this first day of intentional foraging, she piled her abundance on the kitchen table. Kama would know what to do next, the mysterious world of canning and jarring and processing fresh produce into food that lasts.

Dune put on a stiff African wax print apron that Kama had worn often. Then she took it off.

How do adults do things? How?

chapter nine

Survivors

After a couple of days of making the most basic vegetable soup recipe on the internet and filling the freezer with it, Dune was stumped and the dining room table was still covered with food.

Mama Vivian's new practice was looking out the window with busy eyes, as if she was reading a scrolling text on the window. She would not turn her head when Dune entered or started talking, responding only to strong drinks.

"You know how to can things?"

No answer.

"It's probably ridiculous. But I don't think we can live off the donations. The stores are emptying out."

Dune rolled Mama Vivian off the bed and stood her grandmother up, wiping her down with a cloth dipped in warm water and baby soap, drying her by patting her with a t-shirt, rubbing lotion into Mama's delicate skin. The wrinkled folds gathered under her grandmother's chin, where her ass met the top of her thigh, at her thumbs. Dune was gentle, lowering Mama into a soft chair. She stripped the used bed pads, checked the sheets, and then layered new pads on top. Once she got Mama back on the bed, as a reward for the hard work, Dune held the straw of a very strong screwdriver up to her grandmother's mouth and waited until the cup was empty.

"Moms knew all these things. I shoulda paid attention."

A connection clicked in Dune's head as she set down the cup, so clear that she started a bit. She checked to see if Mama Vivian had spoken the suggestion, but her grandmother was looking out the window again. Dune left her to the blurred stupor without a goodbye.

Dune had barely come in the living room since Mama Vivian had relegated herself up to the bedroom. She rushed into it now, heading for what Kama had called the "library," a nook of built-in bookshelves at the back end of the living room. Scanning the walls of books, Dune was impressed by Kama's self-directed PhD-level courses, organized alphabetically by topic, shelf after shelf.

What she sought was on the end wall—two sagging shelves of books on cooking. Brendon had teased Kama for these books, "Really Comet? Who needs a book on sauces? A pamphlet on strawberry jam?" He believed cooking was learned by being in the kitchen with a cook. But Kama had grown up in a household where the kitchen was more of a danger zone than a classroom, so, like everything else, she'd taught herself.

The Ball Blue Book of Canning.
The Joy of Pickling.
Saving the Season.
The Art of Fermentation.
Preserving Memories.

Kama and Brendon had been information-driven—they both

loved to speak in facts, making cases to each other by referencing history and statistics. Dune knew this wasn't the kind of person she was. Kama had read all these books, known all these facts, these ways of doing things right. Brendon had loved comparing texts, and Mama Vivian had done philosophical translation.

Dune had avoided things that relied on book learning, considered herself a student of lived experiences.

Now she pulled *The Ball* book off the shelf. There was no one left to guide her through this experience. Dune had no choice but to do things differently than she'd ever done them before.

....

Dune stumbled out of Kama's room, trying hard to hold her head steady. She'd fallen asleep to the fog of a couple of stiff McCallan's and now she felt resentful that alcohol left this kind of rubble inside her head. She needed water. She made a promise to herself to drink whiskey slowly from now on, with water. As she said it, some part of her knew it wouldn't happen. She liked the dizzy numbness that came from rapid fire shots. She stepped into the kitchen and suddenly felt so alert that the hair on her arms stood up, her head cleared.

The harvest on the table had been organized. As she'd brought home vegetables over the last few days, she had just spilled things onto the table, to come back and work on once she figured out what everything was. Now the abundance was in a circle of ordered piles around the table. In the middle, one of the books was open.

Had she gotten drunk and organized these vegetables?

She stepped up to the table, touching the book. It was open to a page that said mustard greens, with photos. Dune looked around the table until she found the pile of mustard greens. The page had information about the nutritional qualities of mustard greens and a set of recommendations for how to cook it. She placed one hand in the book to save the page, and gingerly lifted the cover until she could see it. *Field Guide to Produce: How to Identify, Select and Prepare Virtually Every Fruit and Vegetable at the Market.* Dune didn't remember finding this book on the shelf, didn't remember being in the kitchen at all last night.

She ran upstairs and peeked in Mama Vivian's room. The pile of dirty sheets she had dropped just outside the door last night was undisturbed and her grandmother had soiled herself. Mama Vivian hadn't done this, then.

Dune took care of her grandmother and then returned to the kitchen and sat down at the table, the raw fuzzy feeling returning to her brain. She would stick to weed for a while. She flipped a page in the book and then another, until she had identified each pile of food on the table and come up with an idea of how she wanted to process it.

She was going to need a lot of mason jars.

chapter ten

Hardware

Approaching the decrepit hardware store on Third with some stealth, Dune tried to remember how long it had been closed. Maybe since the big Ace Hardware store came over on Trumbull? Seemed like a long time. But some places never looked open.

She knocked on the front door, waited long enough for an answer, if one was coming. The quiet inside the store matched that of the city around it.

She walked her bike around to the back of the building and rested it against a concrete wall facing a field of yellow dandelions. The flowers bloomed all the way to the upper edge of the enclosed highway everyone called the Lodge. It was strangely warm today, and Dune tied her hoodie around her waist before trying to figure out how to get into the small building. There was one door along the back, under a row of dusty windows that were too high for anyone to look inside.

Dune knocked again back here and then jiggled at the door knob. It was locked, but there was no padlock or chain. The door looked weak, the wood warped and swollen. She kicked at it a few times and felt the wood give a bit. Then she ran and smashed herself against it and the door exploded inwards. She crashed onto a floor spattered with old paint and felt a bruise begin on her shoulder. With her foot she pushed the door closed behind her and lay on her back for a minute, letting her eyes adjust to the shadows. The air felt thick.

She stood up and pulled herself together in the messy back hall of the store, regaining her balance and breath between the shelves of floor to ceiling hardware. There was no discernible order to all the things the shelves held up and the shelves themselves were under the agreements of no obvious gravity. Her gut was tense, her body wanted to get out of here. Person, rat, ghost—she was equally frightened of each option appearing in this hidden place. What if she got sick in here? Would anyone ever find her?

Just get what you need and go. She pushed herself to move, bringing her mind away from the image of herself wasting away in the darkness of this abandoned heap.

She slid through and into the soft light of the store, list in her head. Jars, lids, tongs, everything the book said she needed to process the food on her table at home.

Everything she touched had a coat of dust on it. Had the dust of her mother slipped in here? Dune wasn't quite sure how dust worked, how it moved. Perhaps her mother was everywhere now. There was no space between thinking of her mother, tearing up, realizing she had tears on her face, moving on. This was normal now.

When she left the store, she exhaled, shaking off the creepiness. She pulled the door behind her, closing it unlocked, hoping she could use the store again if she needed, open to others getting what they needed too. She couldn't get the box of mason jars to balance on her bike without holding it in place, so she walked the bike home.

The first vegetable soup she'd made was solid, hearty, big chunks of potatoes, carrots and other root vegetables in the broth. Next she followed the instructions for cooking and canning a pureed corn soup and then an arrabiata sauce. Dune got twelve jars canned and was excited by how many things wouldn't need refrigeration if she canned them properly.

It wasn't until the third day of her food processing experiments that Dune realized she wasn't just dabbling in disaster prepared-ness—she was preparing for the coming winter. It was obvious once she let herself think it.

She didn't trust the city to get them through and she wasn't going anywhere. She thought she could prepare enough food to get her and her grandmother through three months, maybe more. If Dune could make this food last through winter, they wouldn't have to leave Detroit.

She went through Kama's office files, which were really just all the flyers and print-outs anyone ever brought to any meeting in Detroit. Most of the paper meant nothing now, but Dune knew Kama had been part of the Food Justice Project and worked on a map of places where food had been grown and sold throughout the city. This copy of the map that Dune found was printed on a fragile piece of pale purple paper. Dune DIY-laminated it, layering clear packing tape edge over edge until this piece of survival gold was enclosed. It felt precious to her.

Kama had been a formidable advocate of gardens and fresh food and Dune knew that there was food all over the city. Every-where she saw a cluster of carrots on the map meant there was a community garden. Many of them were behind fences, but fences meant less and less to Dune each day.

She learned that the little snowflakes meant cold storage when she came across a few cartons of potatoes in a subtle root cellar at a community garden a mile away. Within hours she'd brought the cartons home and processed them into future french fries and tall mason jars of potato soup, some with rosemary and garlic, others with leeks and celery. She stored the jars on the other side of the basement and took gallon bags of fries to the deep freezer in the shed.

The gardens were the priority. At the rate the city was emptying there wouldn't be enough people left to take care of all that land. She wondered how much she could manage and if she could figure out what to do with all the food. The task felt impossible, which made her miss Kama, mother of all the plans and none of the fruition, who somehow excelled at the random and impossible task.

chapter eleven

Choosing to Stay

All across the city, people were making the choice to wait the syndrome out. They were all using different strategies to avoid H-8, none of them grounded in solid proof that they worked.

There was a group that felt they were being left behind in a rapture. Their theory was that everyone was misinterpreting the faces of those who became sick—that it was not grief but overwhelm in the face of the divine. One by one, Detroiters were being awestruck, leaving behind their earthly bodies. This group met up at Hope Community Church, weekly at first, then daily as work fell away. From there they would journey together around the city, looking for sick people. When they found one who was out in public, unclaimed, they would hold hands with each other, and then place hands on them and begin to pray. They prayed to be seen in their devotion, loving this neighbor and each other. They professed, again and again, their faith: Jesus came, Jesus gave his life for us, Jesus was the only son of God. They prayed in ripples of whispers and shouts, taking turns at the heart of the collective supplication, waiting to be blessed with the invitation to the other side.

Another group wore face masks everywhere they went, even when they slept, certain that there was something borne on the air itself, some particle, some fleck of death that simply needed to find its way into the lungs of a breather to infect them. They passed out flyers on the distinctions between surgical masks and the Q498 masks that were "actually safe." They went to all the city meetings, advocating that industrial respirators should be made available to everyone still in the city limits.

A smaller circle had split off from the masked ones, a group that felt it was significant that the lungs were being targeted, as the belief in Chinese medicine was that the lungs actually hold grief. All of those struck with H-8 looked like humans in an advanced stage of grief. They wore the face masks too, but spent the bulk of their time in grieving rituals, convinced that, if they could face their grief, process it together, they would survive the syndrome. They approached the sick with mantras, "Go easy in your grief, we are the ones who suffer."

The anarchists wore bandanas and harvested food from gardens all over the city, working in crews of three or five. They set up a headquarters in the Living Arts building in Mexicantown; several of them slept there, not wanting to risk dying alone. They partnered with the Honeybee Market, working as cashiers and stocking food, meeting vendors at the 75 South checkpoint to bring in fresher produce. When people got H-8 they walked them down the street to the clinic. They didn't have life support capacities, but there was a team there who would work to slowly get water and broth into the bodies of the sick.

Some people were like Dune, they thought it best to burn the bodies of the sick. But there was a small contingent that felt it was important that the bodies actually left the city. Getting sick and dead people past the checkpoints was a no go. To clear the sickness from the city, these believers would wait until the dead of night and take their corpses down to the river in cars with the lights turned off. If they made it, avoiding the patrols and police, they would slide the bodies over the railing, down into the river.

The *Michigan Citizen* was more of-the-people than most publications, but only available online these days. They kept publishing a weekly list of people who were known to have died after contracting H-8, alongside news of relief efforts, reporting on theories about the syndrome, and opinion pieces on how the city was mishandling the crisis.

Dune suspected that, regardless of strategy, most of these people—faithful, rebellious, reporting, grieving—would not last the winter. Not because they were right or wrong, but because they were there, in Detroit, and H-8 was an indiscriminate hunger that the city needed to slake.

....

Dune would have told anyone who asked that she didn't believe Kama had contracted anything. Her mind had just quit one day, in an apparent overwhelm of ... frustration? Sadness?

No one asked. Or more accurately, perhaps they gave up on trying to ask while Dune was in the initial throes of grief behind her closed door. Perhaps by now they had forgotten about Kama and Dune in the chaos of H-8, which had touched everyone in the city in some way.

Calling whatever had taken her mother away a syndrome, specifically "Syndrome H-8," had given Dune the impression that there was a clear, known set of symptoms, something trackable, and, perhaps eventually, avoidable. Dune found herself wondering, what was H-7? Or C-3 for that matter? What were the names of the syndromes before this? How did they relate to these symptoms? Did the letters mean something, was it pure categorization? Who named syndromes like this? Had there been others like this? Had she missed some rash of random, fatal, place-based syndromes?

She imagined a group of skinny white boys with glasses and doctor coats on, playing Operation. Where did H-8 live in the body? Was the H for humanoid, hack, hell? Hate, harm, holocaust? Was this the eighth cleansing of the earth? The eighth level of inferno?

As the weather cooled, Dune found herself drawn to the syndrome like an ambulance to a wreck. The first time she noticed the list in the *Citizen*, she added the names to the model, at whatever address was listed. After a few weeks of this, she decided to see what she could find out about these new ghosts. She mapped the addresses and started to tour the tombs on her food runs.

Part of her needed to see the homes, see if they looked at all like hers—were they painted gold? Two floors? Was there an abandoned apartment building nearby? Was there a pattern in terms of what was growing around the home—fatal chicory? Were they at the same proximity to water, or the incinerator, or old factories, or other homes? Did the houses seem to droop an inch with sorrow?

Theories rooted and dispersed in her, dandelions seeking proof and then, poof, on the wind.

Summer and fall were usually Detroit's outdoor seasons, long days full of Black people outside blasting music, seeing and being seen; biking with or without bike lanes, walking and loitering on sidewalks, shopping at farmers markets, out on their boats, working all day long. The city soundscape uplifted its own creative children, boomboxes competing as soul wrapped around rap up against techno, strolling through jazz—all swallowing petty pop as cultures did subtle battle for the city's surface.

Dune felt the dearth of people, that familiar flow of strangers that had made the river of sound and life around her. Now everyone she met was like her, a droplet falling a great distance, certain to crash land at some point, to become a part of the flood.

When, occasionally, she would cross the path of someone still sentient and willing to stand apart and share information, she began to ask questions of the survivors: How many have you lost? Was he looking out a window when it happened? Was she alone? Or were you there? Did she say anything after she got sick, words, murmurs? Were they crying? What are you going to do with them? What happened to them?

Sometimes it was too soon to be asking anything. She would learn this in the conversation, when the griever before her would come out of their shock enough to get angry with her, usually three or four questions in. She didn't take it on. They were angry at what had happened and she only had questions, no answers.

One morning, agitation pushed her to flip through the stack of papers on the mail table until she found the slip of paper where she'd written Dr. Roger's phone number down. She called it. Someone picked up the phone, but didn't seem to speak. They breathed together, strangers. Eventually Dune broke the silence, "Hello?"

"Yes. Hi."

"Dr. Rogers?"

"I am she." The doctor sounded tired.

"This is Dune Chin—"

"Oh," a spark of life. "Kama's daughter? Yes, I remember you! I ... how *are* you?"

"Uh. Ok I guess. I've been researching H-8 since my mom died. And. I was wondering what you were able to learn about it."

"Ah. Yes. Well first I really want to apologize to you Dune. There's really no excuse, this is the most devastating part of being a doctor, having no room to help people because of the way the medical system is set up in terms of insurance. So many random situations come through. You never know when something odd is actually something new. I doubt we could have saved your mother, I want to say that. But you shouldn't have had to care for her like that. Bury her like that. I am sorry."

"Thank you." Dune was surprised to realize that Dr. Rogers knew what had happened here, had been paying some attention to her through this time. "I hear that. But, I'm curious. Do you still think she was patient zero?"

"I do. Everyone who survived that first wave agrees. Whatever it was, is, it touched Kama first. Though she wasn't the first to die."

"Is it only us—Black people, people with African ancestry?"

"I am not at liberty to affirm that." Heavy pause. "By telephone."

"Oh." Dune thought into the silence for a second. "Where *could* you affirm that?"

"You're on Second, near Brainard?"

"I am."

"Go to Jumbo's."

Dune saw the green windowless brick of a bar in her mind, chained up for months now. "OK."

The phone buzzed with completion and Dune felt a flurry in her belly—curiosity tinged with fear, or vice versa. She was going, but she thought it was most likely a trap. Her only nego-tiating leverage was that Mama Vivian was here and needed her to return.

Then she caught her racing and suspicious mind. Whose trap? Leverage for what? And with who?

She resolved again to take a break from weed.

....

The mural was on the parking lot side of the evergreen building, lush bright flowers unfolding around ringed witchy hands. Dune leaned against the wall near the back of the lot, close to the alley that would take her home if things looked shady and escape was an option. She heard a vehicle park nearby, and then Dr. Rogers came walking around the corner, crossing the gravel lot.

Dune stayed easy, let the doctor approach. She didn't look like Dune remembered or expected, her face was a soft worn brown, eyes gentle, fatigued and inquisitive above her mask. The doctor said hello with open palms, waiting, as if Dune had initiated this meeting.

"Why you still here?"

"I'm actually leaving tomorrow," Dr. Rogers answered, with an intense, invitational gaze. "I was supposed to evacuate weeks ago, but the research is here."

"But why—"

"To talk to you." The doctor's smile tipped left, as if she were embarrassed. "And the others who were in that first wave of survi-vors. You're the last one still here. Dune, I've never seen anything like this. I've been reading everything I can get my hands on. This H-8 has no biological precedent."

"So it's a brand new disease?"

"I'm not convinced it's a disease at all. Like a virus is genetic code, it infects the cells and kills the host. Initially we were careful to refer to this only as a syndrome, a group of associated symptoms... The symptoms align with extreme traumatic shock, even some of the negative symptoms of trauma induced psychosis—comparable to when people lose everything in a sudden act of war or manmade disaster. The system can become so overwhelmed that it shuts down, reducing to only core functions for a period of time. But there's no war here. No disaster. Just an average day in Detroit."

Dune blinked and in that instant her mother's elusive last words came flooding back into her memory, *"The economics are heartbreaking. Every day is a war here! On our dignity! On our humanity! We out here trying to wage love, wage love in a war against people breaking the main tool we have. Our hearts can't take it! My heart can't—"*

She blinked back into the present at Dr. Rogers's touch, the slender Black hand extended in comfort, or concern. Dune pulled away sharply, and then felt guilty.

"If it's not a disease ... like ... what *is* this?"

Dr. Rogers rubbed at her bleary eyes. "I don't know. I'm trying to figure this out. Every way I can think of answering that sounds certifiable. But be careful, Dune. I think someone wants us gone. And there's almost no one left to fight."

"Us?"

"Black people. H-8 takes Black people out of ourselves. To... grieve?"

They stood together, quiet, feeling the tender logic in the mystery. Of course Black people were dying from grief. But why now? Why here?

They spoke a while longer, until there was almost nothing left to say. Dune pushed off the wall to head home, dissatisfied and agitated, wanting to write down what she had remembered from her mother's mouth before it disappeared again.

"Dune. One more question."

"What's up."

"This is a bit awkward." The grimace on the kind doctor's face was a warning. "Where did you cremate your mother?"

"Why?"

"I'd—it would be helpful to see if there's any organic matter still there. I could continue my testing that way. I have several samples from people who came later in the process, but, she's patient zero."

Dune wanted to say no, to lie, to deny this unreasonable request. She glared away from the doctor for a full minute. Then she told Dr. Rogers to come with her and wait on the porch. Dune removed two of her mother's finger bones from the bed altar. She wrapped them in one of Kama's endless bonnets and brought this offering to science outside. Dr. Rogers didn't ask any questions, but looked at Dune with more respect, more sadness. When they said goodbye, Dune was sure it was the last time.

....

Song for Vivian. (Sung at pace of a dirge, with lots of mournful melisma.)

Where is the silent place
The silence so full it cannot stop
It's under us all when down we drop
Its under every face

What is the freedom road
When all the warriors have gone home
When all the healers sleep alone
Who else will bear this load

How does the galaxy
Hold all this pain and not knowing
Hold all this pain and keep glowing
Who am I meant to be

chapter twelve

The Syndrome and the Model

After the disappointment of learning Dr. Rogers didn't really know more than anyone else about H-8, Dune's expectations dropped for the others left behind by the sick. They were all as ignorant and sad as her, and she didn't need heartbroken conjecture. She also started to pay more attention to those who were sick.

At first it had been too much, pulling her right back to Kama. But she began to see these other sick people as part of a community that included Kama. These people, rocking in the middle of the street, had perhaps seen something that her mother had seen and Dune had not.

What was it?

At first it was hard to tell the sick from every other affliction or coping mechanism. Public intoxication and highness had increased in the face of H-8.

But Dune noticed that when folks were high, drunk, even having a moment of madness, there was often a look of comfort on their faces. She understood it, often looking at them through the gentle haze of her own high. Pain was real and life was suffering, but they had found a moment's respite, a warm belly, a sense of belonging, a blurring of the sharp edges of a world that rejected them for being who they were—Black, veteran, poor, rebellious, spiritual, pregnant too early, loving too hard, wounded by the world.

There was medicinal peace and they could dose themselves with it.

H-8 had a different effect. Dune tried to pinpoint it—the first thing she knew was that it produced a reaction in her body, a chill, a goose-pimpling of her skin. There was a deeper stillness, a giving up way down in the nervous system. The look on the faces of the sick was usually somewhere between horror and immense longing, the way the word "why" looks when something precious and irreplaceable dies.

She had nothing to offer but her witness to these moments in people's lives. Possibly the worst moments, although she had never felt comfortable assuming death was worse than life. Who knew what awaited them? Were the days or weeks of sickness purgatory? Was it a feeling of being trapped deep inside oneself as she'd dreamt more than once now? Or was the spirit far off already?

Slowly, approaching person by person, sick or well, Dune felt her own fear fall away. She kept moving close to H-8 and surviving. She didn't take this for granted. It felt important that she kept surviving, like an emergent responsibility. It emboldened her to move closer, to learn more.

Dune was frustrated by the lack of clarity her "research" yielded. She wanted an answer, or at least a solid clue. She needed theories to explore beyond official variations of "What the fuck?"

....

A week or so after the visit with Dr. Rogers, Dune woke up frozen, in a panic again, and had to find her way back into control of her body. She didn't think this was H-8, though she wondered if maybe she was patient zero for some variation that created this horrible phase of conscious sedation before returning to the body.

After she had blinked, breathed, shaken herself out of the ice, she had a thought that made her panic: Maybe she wasn't Black enough to get H-8.

She had been right there in the room with her mother. Gone to the hospital, gone to the store, taken no real precautions besides a mask that she wore intermittently. She was grieving, she was sad, she was scared ... but she wasn't sick. She kept not getting sick. Why? What sick logic was sparing her from this syndrome?

Kama had always told Dune, "You are Black. Black plus Chinese, yes, but Black." Chinese ancestry notwithstanding, Kama wanted Dune to always know her Blackness as the first nonnegotiable aspect of who she was. "Every light-skinned Black person comes from a lineage of dark-skinned Black people and something else. For a lot of them, that light skin was a wound, from an act of violence and domination. And for a lot of us, every day, whiteness tries to make light skin wound the rest of us. But for you? You come from a love story. You come from two lineages of oppressed peoples who found love with each other. I love your daddy, we both free, and I have raised you to know your Black story and B has raised you to know your Chinese story. But there's no world in which people would see you and just say, oh she's Chinese. There's no world in which they would see you and think you ain't Black. You ain't half of nothing. You Black." Dune had never felt less-than in Kama's presence.

But now she looked in the mirror, wondering if Kama's loving miscegenation had produced a child who wasn't Black enough to die with her people. And that thought made her breath catch again, a different kind of cold prickling her spine.

....

Every day now, Dune would get up, take care of Mama Vivian, and then leave the old woman to her own quiet company.

She wasn't angry with her grandmother, but she didn't have the patience to sit there yelling to herself, sharing news of the nothing that was spreading outside. The only time she felt connected to Mama Vivian was when she sang to her.

Dune was grateful for Bab, who visited several times a week now. Bab approached keeping Vivian company with the same steadiness that Dune approached demystifying H-8. They sometimes passed in the hall, heading towards their chosen apocalypse work.

Dune went out looking for encounters all hours, first thing in the morning, at sunset, by moonlight. She was surprised by how many people came out at night. Perhaps they were ashamed to have neighbors see that their houses were touched by the sickness? Perhaps they, like her, thought that their fragile, grief-stricken states would come to less harm in the dark? She wondered if some of her neighbors were leaving their sick outside at night.

At this point the question for those who stayed wasn't "has H-8 taken someone from you," but "how many? How close? How often?"

Detroit is a small town in a big city's dress. Dune felt a deeper, stranger intimacy emerge as the numbers of living people dwindled. Those who stayed all walked with their ghosts at hand.

She biked the streets, stopping by emergency rooms, eyes peeled. Dune became a field researcher. She carried a soft cover notebook, blank inside. She filled the pages with as much information as she could gather, beginning to fear that any single thing she missed would be the lost key to the whole crisis.

The first thing she noticed as she got closer was the words. Just like Kama, most of the sick peoples' mouths were moving.

Dune hadn't tried to decipher the words Kama was saying in the two weeks of watching her die. She had been focused on getting some kind of liquids into her mother. Now that she remembered her mother's diatribe in the kitchen, Dune was racking her brain, sure that she could find her mother's repeated words in the folds of memory matter. Now, when she came across a sick person, she wasted no attention on the assumption that she could save them. Now, instead, she listened.

．．．．．．．．．．．．．．．．．．．．．．．．．．．．．．．．

Field notes:

Black, masculine, over six feet, red polo shirt (stained at armpits—sweating in this chill?), jeans w/torn out knees (he's dressed for a quick dash outside), purple skully, gray hoodie. Standing in the field/lot at the top of the Dequindre Cut off Gratiot. Words, at least 5, what I could understand was: "winning tigers." October 3.

Four members of one family, Black/Afrolatinx, in waiting room at Henry Ford. Brought in by wife/mother, with two surviving children waiting in car. Sick: father and three children, ages 49, 16, 12, 9, names Rocky, Sandra, Sasha and Sara. Last name Jefferson. Children are quiet, man is vocal but incoherent (cooing, almost comforting noises). Wife said they live between Chene and St Aubin on Leland St, and all got sick within two days of each other, starting with the father. Hysterical, wouldn't let me see or speak to her other two children. She wants to know if they can be protected, if it's genetic. Left sick family members at hospital for observation. Car with other two children in back, full of luggage. October 7.

Young Black/maybe mixed, maybe early 20s? In field on Mack close to Rosa Parks. Wearing a belted green dress, long black hair with red highlights. She is the lightest skinned person I have seen with H-8, (lighter than me). Stylish, student? Artist? Saying "my heart" or "my art" over and over. Soiled, been there a while. October 18.

With each person she found, Dune would write her notes down and then, if they were alone, she would call 911 and report their location for pick up. Dune took off before the police could get there, not interested in the urgent conversations full of questions with no answer. She wouldn't be able to help the popo in their useless interrogations, even if she weren't opposed to their existence. Which she was.

She would take these sick humans home with her as facts, descriptions, words, locations and dates. She would walk into her home, hang her coat in the hall, slide out of her boots; and check on her grandmother, changing the diapers, wiping the shit, refilling the screwdriver mug, and kissing the forehead. Then she would descend to the basement to create memorials, just as she'd done for Kama. She would make a little sign for each person and place it in her father's model of the city, as close as she could get to the place they had become sick.

She had almost four hundred names now. Hardly a tenth of the total crisis. She wouldn't forget them, she wouldn't let them simply disappear.

....

Dune was hungover again, slowly heading down the stairs. It wasn't a good biking day when her head felt like this. She waved two fingers at Bab, who was dropping off a loaf of homemade bread on the table, then storing a tin of fresh butter in the fridge. Bab nodded amicably and made her way upstairs.

Bab was visiting daily now. Dune tried to be away or in the basement. She was grateful for Mama Vivian to have some company, grateful for the extra hands giving her grandmother care. But she didn't want the small talk, didn't need it.

She was pretty sure it helped Bab more than anyone else. She came, cried and yelled to Mama Vivian about the crisis and what she imagined Mama Vivian might think about it. Dune listened until she heard the one-sided rhythm of sound. Bab was great at filling the space with Vivian, as if she had stored up small stories her entire life. Dune slipped down into the basement, wanting to be quiet, alone. She had to add the week's names to the model and wanted to find a way to keep track of the houses she still needed to follow up on. Creating systems was beginning to feel as comforting to her as smoking weed, it was something tangible and instantaneous, something reliable.

After a couple of hours, Dune came back up, pleased with her map for the next day's investigation. She made herself a slice of bread slathered in the fresh butter, realizing it was her first food of the day. She cut off another slice and ate it as she stood at the bottom of the stairs. When she was sure she didn't hear anything, she climbed the stairs to check on Mama Vivian.

Her grandmother was laying there with terror in her eyes. Bab was sitting in the guest chair on the far side of the bed, staring off at the wall, her face gone to torment, tears dripping in a soft swinging motion from her petite pointed chin and damp in her sparse locs.

Dune dropped the bread and ran over to check Mama Vivian's responses. Her grandmother was still here and she looked so confused, trying to understand what was happening. Dune hoped for small blessings—that Bab had just turned, not been sitting like this for hours. That she hadn't wet herself. That she was movable.

Dune pulled Bab to standing and was grateful that she could shuffle her off down the hallway. Dune returned and gave Mama Vivian water, apologizing over and over, even though there was nothing any of them could do. H-8 wasn't her fault.

Dune drove Bab home, escort to a quiet ghost. Bab had no words, which surprised Dune at first, though maybe she had spoken them all in these months of caring for Vivian. Bab's roommates, a crew of older people of color who might all be lovers, were still there to receive her, another small blessing. Dune knew that in bringing their friend back to them, she was devastating their home.

They all knew about Kama and offered condolences, but in their shock, no one asked anything else. Dune was relieved.

When she returned to the house she sat by her grandmother's bed, holding Mama Vivian's hand. She told her grandmother that they wouldn't see Bab again and that it was the same thing that had happened to Kama. She didn't know what else to say. The emotion of earlier had left Mama's face and Dune couldn't tell if anything was getting through.

....

Most of Dune's days now consisted of bizarre firsts.

Like the first time she realized that someone had left a sick person in a boarded-up home. She'd been across town to see about a community garden behind a church in Brightmoor and was on her way home. It was a glorious Detroit sunset that night, wide and bright, softening into a purple dusk. She'd seen a home with a front window cracked open next to a boarded-up door. The rest of the windows were boarded up too. She wondered, *what was the point*, and then it struck her so hard she hit the brakes.

A just-in-case option? Even though no one who had gotten sick had recovered at all, much less enough to walk out of their homes.

She had jumped out of the car and gone right up to the open window, ducking down to look in. And there, in the last fading light of day, she could see a knee, someone sitting in the room past the living room, maybe a dining room? She called out several times, but the knee didn't move. No one else responded, no other sounds came from within. She tried to get her courage up to slip in, gather more data on the owner of the knee.

She couldn't though. It was nearly dark. And even though the line between sick and dead was negligible these days, she wasn't really ready to meet a dead stranger in the dark. And what if someone else had gone in the open window already and felt defensive about the territory?

Dune wrote down the notes she could from the window: *brown hand on knee, looks like an older man's hand. Black pants.* She got the address, the date. That would have to do. She sat in her car for a long time before she could pull off, feeling like a coward.

....

It was Halloween.

She went in her parents' office, moving down through the small closet until she found a dusty box that said HOLIDAY in block letters down the side. Soon, half her face was painted like a grinning white skeleton. She went upstairs and made teasing eyebrows at Mama Vivian.

"If this isn't our day, I don't know what is," she said.

She painted her grandmother's face, moving the brush softly, slowly over the elder's skin. Did Vivian nearly smile?

Dune slipped close to Mama Vivian and took a picture of the two of them. She didn't know who to share it with, but was happy to have it.

Half-masked, she continued with a regular day.

She made black beans and oatmeal for breakfast. She thought of the breakfasts she wanted. Real eggs, fried over medium with sea salt and pepper. With bacon, and chicken apple sausages, smoked salmon, buttered toast, all of it smothered in hollandaise. And french toast and pancakes, quiche, frittata, things that came with and from eggs.

She needed to find some chickens come spring, maybe from Ohio if she could get past the quarantine boundary. Twice. "Going rogue."

She checked Mama Vivian's adult diaper. She had initially felt guilt at not doing this until after breakfast, making her grandmother sit in it, but the truth was she couldn't eat for a while afterwards. Mama Vivian would barely swallow water or Ensure now. She loved the screwdrivers still, but she didn't have much waste to process these days.

Dune went about her chores and tasks feeling a deep exhaustion, a soreness in her joints. Her body's changing weight was equal parts comforting and taxing on her skeleton. At the end of the day, she drew a very hot bath, hissed her way down into it and sat, feeling her pores open up, releasing everything. Her mask melted off, floating white on the water's surface around her. She dried her hands on a towel from the floor and picked up the top book on the pile next to the tub, flipping pages until the water was cool.

She'd finished all the cookbooks. Now she was slowly reading every book of philosophy in this house. Hegel, Davis, Tolle, Boggs. It was a way to be close to her parents, immersing herself in these books that had given direction to Brendon's life, lived verbatim in Kama's mind.

Sometimes what she read was clear to her, other times the words blurred together, became sounds in her head. This still comforted her, because they were human words, and it had the effect of hearing her parents speaking in the next room, lulling her down towards sleep.

Tonight, words on the Russian revolution calmed her, reminded her of how proud Mama Vivian was that humans had done such a thing.

She dragged herself, wrapped in a towel, to the bed at the front of the hall. Tomorrow she would unmask her grandmother.

....

Dune had to evolve what she was doing, what she was looking for. Again.

She went back for Mr. Knee, this time at peak daylight. Feet first, through the window into the living room. The house had been trashed since she'd been there two nights before, but no one had touched Mr. Knee. He was still breathing, but likely not for long. She apologized to him, though she wasn't sure for what exactly—his abandonment? His having to sit through the robbery of his home? Her own cowardice? Her presence at his last moments?

She promised him he wouldn't be forgotten.

After Mr. Knee, Dune took the time to look through windows for survivors. Then she started breaking into places where she was sure there were people inside. She was rarely wrong.

She understood the true scale of the crisis in this way, by all of the people she found who weren't being taken anywhere, hooked up to any life support. The wealthy minority had been struck by the crisis of H-8, but they had left as soon as they believed it was happening. So many people couldn't afford to go. Couldn't afford to do anything for their loved ones. Like her, they had to watch their loved ones die. Unlike her, they didn't risk staying, risk that death themselves.

She grieved with the people who had to leave their loved ones like this. She grieved for the people left in the dark houses, or left beside one light in an otherwise dark house, or left inside of houses boarded up with all the lights on, warm air blowing.

....

The house smelled. She was about five feet from the closed door. There was a window just right of the door and it was wide open with a screen, but it was too cold for open windows at night now.

Another just-in-case house.

She covered her nose and marked it with her sharpie on the door. She'd learned the hard way that most of the just-in-case houses were tombs for dead people. She was surprised at how strong the rotting scent was even in the cool air, was grateful for the warnings the smells provided, even when they turned her stomach.

There weren't always smells. She found newly dead people in beds, slumped over tables, in piles in the kitchen, almost always alone. She found dead people who had obviously committed suicide, in bloody tubs, sleeping forever next to empty pill bottles, collapsed in armchairs with holes through their heads, their final thoughts strewn across the wall.

She learned what made her retch and what she could look past.

She found lots of notes and journals. She always left them. That was outside her field of study, beyond her emotional reach.

She wasn't the only one searching houses—the CDC had a task force mostly focused downtown, going apartment by apartment. Because of them, she had spent three nights boarding up the lower windows on her house. Because of them she only used the back entrance these days, off the back alley. Because of them her home became truly circadian.

Dune's father had been obsessed with New Orleans after Katrina, fascinated by the codes they used to communicate about the living and the dead in their watermarked city. He and Kama had a photo album from their visit there as a sister city delegation, and he'd shown it to Dune when she was doing a climate justice report in the sixth grade.

Now, conjuring her father's collaboration, she came up with a similar system of marking the houses of the dead in Detroit. A circle, halved, with a number on top for the dead person or, occasionally, people, found inside. The bottom half was the date she'd found them. If she found pets inside, she liberated them and also noted that. Her marks were small, visible only once you knew to look.

She began to see the city through this tiny new pattern. It reminded her of Tyree Guyton's Heidelberg Project. For years, Tyree had marked solid pastel circles on Detroit buildings that he felt should have been demolished before his father's childhood home, protest art.

She did enough research to know that decomposition takes a really long time and decided not to even attempt to forage these houses for at least six months, maybe a year.

Such long-term thoughts. What was she resigning herself to?

chapter thirteen

Two Graveyards

Dune was biking down Mount Elliott. It was the first truly cold day outside, frost on the grass. She could feel the air on her earlobes and jaw. She wouldn't be able to bike much longer.

She slowed down as she approached the cemetery.

This close to the territory of death, all of those tombstones, planted flowers raising up, decaying flowers laying sideways, she felt a certain kinship.

She wondered about the first time someone had needed a graveyard—not just a burial ground for family, but something larger, for members of a community, village, church. It must have been a moment like this, a deluge of bodies, dead in some mysterious way.

Otherwise, everyone could do what she had done, handle their own dead. An article crossed her mind, she thought it was *Tricycle* magazine, a story about Buddhists cleaning their dead and Hindus floating their flaming beloveds' corpses into a sacred river on pyres. Perhaps it was a whole issue on death.

She paused, propping herself up with a foot on the curb, to make a note to research this. There were many notes like this now, starred questions and directives. It was satisfying to know that some questions had answers, some tasks could be completed.

She cut into the cemetery at the gate, biking between the stones. Yes, she thought, a public graveyard would have to be a mathematical imperative. War, plague. She thought of the bone border in Palestine, where the Israelis had had to relinquish so much territory under international pressure, but refused to let the Palestinians gather the remains of their warriors from the seventy-four-year occupation. The same thing was happening between the US and Mexico. She couldn't see how war today was any less barbaric than Europeans placing heads on spikes, or the genocidal ashes in Germany that left behind piles of shoes and watches and dental fillings. Piles of skulls in Rwanda, Khmer Rouge; the Parisian catacombs. Dune wondered if the source of destruction mattered once you could build structures of skeletons.

When would this place be ready for catacombs? The city was already somewhere between an emergency room and a graveyard.

She coasted out of the cemetery, heading towards the checkpoint on Jefferson. People crossing out of the city there were heading north along the water, to drive west across the state, or keep going to the Upper Peninsula, sometimes to continue over into Wisconsin.

Moving between the houses, she was struck by how, even in the onslaught of death, humans protected their belongings. She wondered if it was an act of resistance—you might take our bodies but you will not take my television. Or my couch.

It seemed so ridiculous to her, to see the houses boarded up daily. Who cared about these things, if you got to leave, alive? If you got the great blessing of driving away with your loved ones? She would leave it all for another hour with Kama.

At this point, survival didn't have to make some greater sense; it didn't have to have an additional purpose. People were leaving behind everything that wasn't flesh, though of course with H-8 most of them left some of that too. Or people were staying, living behind gas masks and prayer. None of it was necessarily logical.

Dune found those departing, approaching with her notebook full of names and stories, her questions and, most of all, her willingness to listen.

An elderly woman wearing pearls, a wide brimmed hat and a pink Sunday dress with a full torso ruffle of lace, stomping in kitten heels, cursed her way down her yard. She was carrying an armload of furs out and seemed to think Dune had come to take the things she couldn't fit in her Cadillac. "At least wait 'til I'm gone!"

Dune hung back without defense.

An attractive couple in their sixties, the Taylors, wore matching track suits and variations on hair loss replacement systems. They were leaving behind their sick daughter with a paid caretaker. They delayed their departure to tell Dune everything about the girl. "Tell them she is a pianist. She knows how to drive the boat. She is our only child. She finished her degree at Clark. She *chose* to come back to Detroit, this isn't fair, she shouldn't even be here. We told her, we told her."

The caretaker wouldn't meet Dune's eyes during the interview. Dune didn't judge.

A young agender artist named Jose was biking to hir next destination and had built a rolling rack for hir earthly belongings, adding a little motor to hir pedals. "I'd love to stay, honestly. Love to. My crew is staying and I bet there are going to be so many stories, inventions. But my sister needs me. And I am not ready to die. Not today."

Dune was a bother to some, a confessional comfort to others, a sort of narrative gravedigger for the people and memories that wouldn't make it past the outgoing checkpoints. She didn't try to soothe anyone, or change their minds. She knew she couldn't play the role of grief counselor to these departing families, so she waved goodbye when the time came. Beyond gathering stories and locations of those they had left behind, she wasn't really focused on the departing, anyway.

They weren't hers. The graveyard was hers. The whole damn city was a graveyard now.

....

They each had a story they wouldn't get to tell. She brought back all of the information she could gather and sat in the basement for hours, organizing it, seeking some clue, some pattern inside the small details.

Not everything fit on her little signs. Dune realized she was unwilling to sacrifice any of her tender data.

She returned to the hardware store, which had definitely been touched by another someone since her last visit, but was unoccupied when she entered and otherwise intact. She was less afraid, but still moved quickly in the spooky half-light, finding index cards, tape, sharpies in different colors, a pack of filing folders. With a bit of guilt, she broke open a cabinet hidden behind a 4x4 piece of lumber where more expensive items were kept, grabbing a handful of ancient hard drives. Dune hoped they would be compatible with one of her parents' computers.

She was making it up as she went now.

Once the supplies were down in the basement, she created a little filing system, numbering each person and matching them with index cards to hold the extended clues, hints, fragments of life. Hundreds of people, thousands of small particles of data, millions of intimacies.

The signs each had the date and address of discovery. The card had the rest of the description. She used pencil if they were sick, and then black ink, black crosses on tiny white flags when she found someone already gone, or when she returned to find a sick person had finished the silent occupation of their own flesh and joined the fully dead. The white and black shapes spread across the model as she circled outward from her home in the center, the virus a spiraling, bleak art.

She briefly wished she had little figurines, but then thought perhaps that would be morbid, stacking dead bodies in the basement. Then again, perhaps this harvest of death data was already a private catacomb, a morbid research.

chapter fourteen

Detroit Red

New snow had dusted the city two days earlier and Dune felt more urgency about finding people, listening, gathering data. The colder it got, the shorter these stolen days would be, the whispering space between life and death.

One night she set out to find flannel sheets for the winter. She thought she could get them quietly if she drove to the suburbs.

That's when she'd seen the woman, facing a house on Outer Drive. Her skin was a faded brown, her short red hair at odds with her coloring. Her neck seemed a bit broken. Her clothing was flamboyant, a short puffy winter coat over a low-cut black mesh dress that had probably once fit perfectly where it now drooped and gathered. She wore high top sneakers with gold wings on them. There was a network of frost on her tights where she had wet herself.

Up close, Dune saw that her wig was askew, that's what gave the initial impression of a broken, useless neck. Dune felt relief seeing it was just the wig, though that didn't change the woman's status as mostly-dead.

The woman was saying, quietly but very clearly, "Juan, home, dance, kiss." She was standing in the walkway of a small one-family house, vines and bushes growing all around it. There was a busted grocery bag at her feet and her trembling arms were still arranged to hold it, her hands gesturing smoothly below the space where the bag had been.

She had an elegance in her hands that drew Dune in, along with the clarity of the words, the pace of repetition.

Dune pulled out her phone and recorded the woman. Then she took several pictures. This woman gave her comfort, it was only the circumstances that were disconcerting. She looked into the windows of the house the woman was facing to see if anyone was in there. No one obvious.

She checked the woman's pockets and purse for keys, and when she found them, it made her sad in a strange way. No one had even tried to take this woman's purse. Theft was at least a form of attention, an interaction. People were so scared or absent that they'd left Red alone here, facing this house long enough to have frighteningly cold skin. None of the keys Red had worked on the front door, so Dune used her own tools to jimmy the lock, feeling a small pride in this skill that made everything accessible.

She pushed Red into the house. Since her mother, she only touched sick strangers when it was absolutely needed—getting them out of the road or the weather. This body had the now-familiar stiffness, but offered no resistance to being moved. There was no commitment, no desire to stay, to go.

Dune made Red wait just inside the door while she moved quietly through the house, checking for dead, for food, for signs of animals. Satisfied that nothing was here to disturb Red's dying, Dune arranged the woman in a high backed leather chair facing the window.

She started to leave, but suddenly felt careless. People shouldn't die like this.

When Dune got home that night, she logged Red into her system. So many people now. And she knew she was barely getting a sliver of the overall numbers of sick people in the city.

Sleeping, waking, eating that whole day, she couldn't get Red off her mind. Maybe that wasn't even Red's home. And she was so coherent. Dune decided to go back and if the woman was still alive, bring her home, or get her to a hospital.

....

In the rearview mirror Red seemed to be intentionally looking away from Dune as they wound their way back into the city center. *Don't take it personally*, Dune thought, that was the angle of her head when she got sick. Turning towards or away was one of the simplest expressions of being alive. Deer turned towards predators, babies turned towards the breast, flowers turned towards the sun. Dune wondered again: what was it that could snatch so much essence out of a person that they were less motivated to survive than a flower?

Pulling up in front of her house, she had no idea what to do with this listless, quiet woman. Dune got out of the car. She'd arranged Red directly behind her, on plastic bags she'd found on the street, hoping to protect her car seats from the ways the woman had soiled herself. Red stood up easily, pliant when pulled. Dune led her up the porch stairs, pulling her legs one at a time up each stair, amazed at how absent any sentience was in this body. She opened the door and brought the woman inside.

Red smelled worse in the enclosed space of the house. Dune took her into the big bathroom, pulled and cut her clothes off and threw them into a garbage bag. She stood Red in the tub and washed her, gently, feeling inappropriate and old as she pressed a warm cloth all over the woman's body until the smells were gone, replaced with sandalwood soap.

Dune went and got one of Mama Vivian's adult diapers and one of Kama's full-length muumuus. After she'd dressed Red and set her up at the kitchen table, she sat down across from her.

Immediately restless, she tried to give Red some water, but quickly saw that this woman wasn't responding like Kama—her mother's swallowing instinct had still worked. Red, the water just poured down her chin. She might have been standing on her own too long. Dune was scared she would drown the woman, defeating the whole purpose of giving this stranger some dignity and company for her death.

Dune finally just sat with Red, whose face hadn't changed at any point in the process. After a few minutes, Red began softly whispering her mantra again, her life words, "Juan. Home, dance, kiss."

Dune had initially been very excited about these words of the sick, but she'd been having a hard time figuring out any patterns in the words. Some people only had one word, all of their existence reduced to one word. But was it the last word they were speaking, or just words they'd spoken often? Or something more poetic, more essential? Was it random, or was it the thing that pushed them into this place? Was it words about the sickness? Was it a way out?

Dune wondered what her own words would be.

....

It wasn't long before she started talking to Red.

"Juan huh? Must have been something. I bet he can feel your love for him, wherever he is." Dune stood up and started making an espresso. Beans from the freezer, ground, unleashing the gorgeous smell, packing the Vesuvio, filling the bottom with water, turning on the burner.

"I was in love. Before Marta hurt me I was so in love with her. And before that I guess I was in love with Ana, like first love type love? Ana was so good. Maybe too good for me." Dune hadn't admitted that before, ever. "And Marta was really beautiful. Is really beautiful, I guess. I don't know where she is. But she was so beautiful, so cool. The cool girl."

"Juan. Home."

"She wouldn't have noticed me in high school I don't think. I wasn't the cute boi you see before you. Not 'til I got older. Ana was more my type really. Nerdy. We spent our time together thinking. I still remember those conversations, you know? Ideas ... Ana didn't believe that humans belonged to each other, or even to a place. She thought we were all meant to be nomadic. But like, all theory. We would talk a lot about how to become more free, inside our little lives." Dune laughed, remembering.

"Dance. Kiss."

"We never even kissed. But Ana's parents loved me, we would sit in her room working next to each other on our computers and then compare our ideas... She never initiated anything in our relationship, I didn't know how. We were like, along for the ride of it. I wish I could combine them, Marta's beauty and passion, Ana's big mind, her humility." Dune smiled, trying to imagine this impossible combination. "Maybe Juan was your combo though. I don't think that is ever going to happen for me."

"Juan, home. Dance. Kiss."

"I'm basically alone now. My mama died, my grandmama is in her last days upstairs. My dad died a long time ago, everyone is dead or leaving. I'm going to stay for a while. So. You're good to be here, you know."

'Til you die. Dune couldn't say it, even if it was the clear truth, even if Red showed no signs of registering anything Dune was saying.

Red was named Bethany Brown according to her wallet, but Dune still called her Red. She talked to Red about love and lessons while she downed her coffee, then made tomorrow's iced tea from chicory and dandelions she'd found in a nearby lot, washed and hung to dry.

Eventually, Dune left Red at the table and went upstairs to check on Mama Vivian. She sat next to her grandmother and contemplated just how alone she was and would be. She resisted it briefly, then surrendered, letting it pass through her, a shudder of something not ready to be a full cry, weaker than that. Mama Vivian was no comfort, she was scarcely a witness.

....

Dune was walking around downtown Detroit.

At the bottom tip of Campus Martius Park, facing the river, she approached an exquisitely old man who was dripping with thick mummified skin. He was sick, but he turned to face her, rocking and crying. He crawled over to her and up, and as he touched her she realized there was a hole through her middle, all the way through, rib to pelvis. He pulled himself up and crawled right through that hole, she could feel his hands heavy and grabbing, his shoulders pressing up against her diaphragm as he pushed through. The tickle of his hair passing out of her, the texture of his flannel shirt brushing against her sensitive innards, she felt everything. He went all the way through but never fell out, never exited. He used her, passing on to some place out of this world.

She leaned forward and looked through herself, red and slippery, and then at the floor behind her, clear through her belly. He was gone and she couldn't see where he'd gone to. Before she could think too much of it, a tiny Black woman was standing before her, sick, weeping in rhythm. She followed the man into, through and beyond Dune.

After that, Dune lost track of the sick people who came to their senses enough to crawl through her.

....

The next morning, Bethany Brown, a stranger, was dead in the living room armchair. Dune let her sit there for a few hours while she scavenged wood and newspaper from around the neighborhood. As she gathered, she decided that the company of others wasn't worth the emotional cost of their cremation. She would move people, help them, be their death companion. But she wouldn't bring them home again and she wouldn't let them die where she had to dispose of them.

She felt along an edge of awareness in her too, the massive distinction between well and sick, the slender shade of difference between sick and dead. Whichever man or god created this demon, they'd raised the question in her: What makes life worth living?

She had one answer: It's more than breath.

chapter fifteen

Quarantine

The realm of the basement was expanding and evolving. Dune couldn't guess or hack her way into Brendon's desktop, so she brought down Kama's old computer to process all the death data.

It wasn't easy—Kama's computer was full. Dune's mother had kept pictures and videos of meetings, events and conversations for some future history book project she hadn't gotten to. Dune didn't want to risk losing anything that belonged to her mother, so she used the old hard drives to hold her growing files. Brendon's color printer allowed her to put the pictures on paper.

She had started taking pictures on her phone in case her descriptions were insufficient, later, if people came back to hear what had happened to their sick. But she found that the pictures had become her company, a way to help her stay in touch with her humanity. The far wall behind the model now watched her work through a few dozen listless eyes.

Mostly she had just written things down in her notebook to transfer into her system in the basement, though sometimes she didn't understand enough to grab out coherent words. When she felt on the brink of understanding people, she made recordings to listen to later, often finding she could hear more without the distraction of their sickness in front of her. These she filed away too. Three or four words sometimes made life stories, if she was willing to fill in the middle ground.

The hardest days were when she could find one word amongst a blur of language, but couldn't decipher the rest. The unfinished stories for the unfinished lives.

She created her systems and then recreated them, adding slips of paper, descriptors, numbers, dates, moving the files around based on geography, chronology. Nothing seemed exactly right, but getting lost in the work *felt* right.

Dune was proud of the intimate portraits she'd been creating of the people she'd found. She felt like an investigative reporter, someone official. She had who, when and where on lock. What, why and how beckoned her into deeper and deeper obsession with the infected.

She had different notebooks—small ones that fit in her pocket, which she took with her into the world, and a thicker unlined book that was partially full of notes, with more and more reflection and journaling. She wrote about how lonely she felt, which felt like such a Marta thing to do. But she found that writing down her feelings, not just what was happening, but how she felt about it, always left her feeling better, clearer, afterwards.

The mold was back. Somehow the model had been mold-free for a decade and now, every time she came down, she was wiping off the thick persistent green, which grew faster and faster, in more places. Her imagination couldn't explore the possible sources of the mold, she felt the cage grief built around her dreams and wonder.

Sometimes the mold defeated her productivity, made her feel done with the outside world, done with the basement, done with others. On those nights, Dune poured a glass of rosé, rolled a spliff and ran a bath. This was a new ritual, concurrently numbing from the inside out and outside in, until feeling wasn't an option.

....

Technically there had been a suggested quarantine since the curfew was imposed, but now that every body of law enforcement was overwhelmed with their own sick and dying, people had been finding ways to leave, occasionally with sick family members in their trunks.

Overnight, the National Guard made the border official with M16s. They set up a Quarantine Station at the airport as the Guard headquarters, someone official determining that that was far enough from the epicenter of the crisis. Concrete barriers were trucked across the Ambassador Bridge and set up with armed checkpoints along 75, 96, 94, Michigan Ave. The tunnel and the Ambassador were already impossible to cross due to customs, the last few years of US paranoia and deportation frenzy having caused Canada (and Mexico) to heighten their security reflexively. Now, every major road that left the city was blocked off, with patrolling guards who would check them on a randomized schedule. A quick fence, more suggestive than prohibitive, was thrown up in a semi-circle that started and ended on the Detroit River.

Detroit had a sprawling, strangely constructed population. While the city was mostly Black, the suburb of Dearborn had the largest Middle Eastern population in the US, there was a long-standing Hmong community, mostly in Hamtramck—one of the small cities inside of Detroit's city limits—and a growing immigrant body in Southwest with families from Mexico, Puerto Rico, El Salvador, Chili, Colombia, Guatemala. All throughout this global community were pockets of Anishnaabe, the first peoples of the region, who still knew it as home.

The white business class came and went as locusts; when times were flush they came to the city and ate everything, then left again to the suburbs during lean years. A lot of them had become obstinate in their suburban living and in the face of the syndrome they went on the defensive, setting up their own police and militia patrols around their stores and gas stations. It was, after all, Michigan, and past that, Ohio, where rural folks generally preferred Black people to stick to the cities, even when they weren't sick.

There were moments of chaos at these new borders. Without much in the way of emergency communication infrastructure in place, a lot of people found out about the boundaries when they tried to cross them. Even with H-8, winter approaching, and no city services functional, there were people left in the city lines, within and beyond the 8 Mile marker.

Detroiters are persistent when it comes to surviving the impossible.

There were seventeen arrests and, finally, one casualty in the first seven days of transition from being an open city to a closed one. The message that people trying to leave without permission would be shot was received, and a new energy set over the city: quiet, but rebellious in it.

On WDET, someone said that there would be a system soon for letting people who were well leave. Those who were left were Black and Brown, elderly or taking care of the elderly, homeless and mostly poor. And each day, they were succumbing to this wild and blameless sickness that looked just like grief.

....

The radio was on when Dune entered the room.

Had Mama Vivian turned it on? If so, it was a small miracle, it meant the old woman had reached over and done something, wanted something. It was a sign of life.

If she hadn't— Dune couldn't quite explain it. And the list of things she couldn't quite explain kept growing. Mama Vivian was the only other person in the house with her, but sometimes the walls felt full.

Dune moved in the small room, gathering glasses crusted with orange pulp, dishes of pureed food that had only given a spoon or two of sustenance to Mama Vivian before she shut her mouth. Dune dusted the surfaces, swept the floor and then helped Mama Vivian migrate to the chair so Dune could change the sheets. Her grandmother smelled of baby powder and urine. While she worked, they listened.

"I don't think it is fair to classify this as a racialized plague, Pat... it is completely unclear at this point if the disease targets African Americans. The city was seventy-six percent African American. Of course the bulk of cases we are seeing reflect the population of the city. Conspiracy theories aren't going to help."

"That is fine for you to say Rick, you aren't Black." Chuckling. "For those of us who are, it is just incredibly suspicious. There are *no* documented cases of H-8 for people who don't have some African lineage, even if it's in the octoroon realm. In the wake of the largest and most impactful protests in the US since the civil rights era, fomented by Black people, we impeach and unseat a race-baiting president, and then we've had the armed attacks, the bombings of Black churches, it's been building into a race war. And then a mysterious syndrome shows up and starts erasing our

Black city of the north? Thinking everything is a coincidence is a privilege."

Dune appreciated the conspiracy theories as much as anything else. All this not knowing was demoralizing. She wanted someone to blame, even if she couldn't generate energy behind it.

"Thanks for coming on Pat, you always broaden the dialogue." It sounded like Pat tried to respond, but Rick continued speaking in a bright cheerful flood and Pat's audio cut out. Dune snuck a glance at Mama Vivian, but couldn't tell if she heard the politics unfolding. "We will keep in touch with you. Now, an update from the Center for Disease Control. Bill?"

"Looking for a cause, looking for a cure. The Center for Disease Control said today that while they have *not* identified a clear cause for Syndrome H-8, there *are* patterns they are observing. Because people have gotten sick in such a high variety of conditions, with the only unifying factor being geography, the best guess is that this disease is highly concentrated, highly toxic and has a short life outside of the body, probably air borne or water borne. The CDC would neither confirm nor deny whether this has anything to do with increased incineration of toxic materials, or local water sources, which many protestors have been pointing to as recently as this past April's riots. At this reporting, while there are cases of people surviving for months on life support, there has been zero recovery. Most people die within two weeks of contraction."

Mama Vivian leaned forward in her chair at that and, for a moment, Dune just knew that her grandmother would speak and that her words would hold some answer. The old woman coughed and sat back, looking down at her hands. Dune smiled her frustration down and offered her grandmother water—how could the old woman know what no one else knew?

chapter sixteen

Rage

Dune spent her days going to emergency rooms and crisis centers and watching, listening, recording her dwindling Detroit neighbors as they left behind their bodies like snake skin. A conscious species was disappearing from the material world. She felt on edge, alive, but existing completely in the interstitial space between life and death. The quiet of Mama Vivian and the city's grievers was a dangerous comfort. She became more attuned to the dying than to the living, shifting on an internal axis.

She biked down to the Wayne State Crisis Center to pick up another week of food donations to supplement what she was able to gather. She also wanted some news, some gossip, even. She was tired of all the sensational outsiders' tales of the doomsday quarantine, tired of hearing nothing about the survivors. She wanted a trustworthy source, a human.

The McGregor building was in the heart of the Wayne State campus, surrounded by deep fountains that had been turned off as long as Dune could remember. When Dune was part of Detroit

Summer, they spent every summer in this building, amongst hundreds of people pursuing liberation in every way at the Allied Media Conference. Learning and teaching radical ways of communicating and living meant Dune trailing Marta to workshops and getting haircuts and tattoos and finding herself in the private release of packed parties... This building was the epicenter for four days each June. The architecture of this building, metal lattice work in diamond shapes, straight lines and open space, had been futuristic once, probably in the fifties. She was intrigued by ideas and images of the future from the past—she was her mother's daughter in this way, carried a name that spoke a future.

Dune joined a line of strangers in sweaters, scarves and rain jackets, all snaked around the huge open atrium. This was by far the most people she had seen together since H-8 arrived.

She realized as she stood there that she needed to pee. She tried to wait it out, but the warmer the room got, the heavier the pressure was inside her. Dune assessed the woman behind her, wondering if she would hold the spot. She was elderly, with cocoa brown skin in a million small folds, wearing a bulky cable knit over a massive sundress that looked homemade. A trustworthy outfit. Dune finally asked for help, fidgeting in place. The elder looked burdened, said, "I guess."

The bathrooms for the public were on the second floor, up a set of stairs that seemed to float between the wall and a slender metal pole up the center. Dune had never relaxed on these stairs, nothing about them felt sturdy. At the top was a square of open balcony hallways that moved around the atrium below like it was an ancient courtyard. The bathroom, straight ahead, aimed for elegance with an old school foyer. A large mirror framed with light-bulbs and leather-topped stools in front of it made it impossible not to see her full length before she got to the stalls. She rushed past herself and peed, exhaling as her body emptied.

Dune hadn't looked at herself much recently. She faced herself briefly on the way out. Her eyes looked different, darker, her face wide and pale, too much time in the basement. Under a new and noticeable belly, her hips rounded out her jeans where they used to fall straight. She dried her hands on her pants as she left.

Dune glanced down at the coiling crowd. She was interested in the clusters, the people who were together. There was a group of Black women standing together, wearing overalls, jeans, boots that could handle some weather, gloves with the finger flesh showing. She wondered where they lived.

There were children down there, not a lot, most on a parents' hip. Most people looked dejected, confused, depressed, pulled deep inside themselves. Dune herself embodied that melancholy. It was easier to see the emotional shape of the crowd from above. As she'd come in she had passed an armed guard, and there was another at the back door. She wondered, again, what they were protecting against. The sickness was either inside them or it wasn't. It couldn't be killed.

On her way back to the stairs Dune looked off to her right and stopped mid-step. At the end of the balcony, a boy was looking out the window, angled away from her. Maybe eight-years-old with ashy, slender, brown limbs extending from a t-shirt and what looked to be swim shorts, massive feet in red high tops, his head too large for his long frail body. He looked stretched thin.

She didn't judge him for being underdressed in this desperate time. It still befuddled Dune that, in spite of the crisis, the season was changing.

When the boy started to rock back and forth she realized he

was sick and felt a little foolish that it had taken her mind a minute to realize what was so obvious in his little body. The boy must have been stationed here while someone watching him got supplies. No one wanted to be near the sick with so much unknown.

Moving closer and around him so that she could see his face, she took in that his vast dark eyes were unfocused, his jaw dropped. She hadn't seen many sick children up close. His lips moved in the soft whisper of H-8, "hashem, toolin'," nothing she could understand. He was so young, he looked like it would be easy to tip him back into the realm of the conscious. Dune stepped closer, trying to understand him better.

"Don't!—don't touch him!" A shout came up from the atrium, someone was pushing through the crowd, racing up the stairs. Dune was already moving back, but when the tiny Black woman got close, she pinned Dune against the wall with her forearm, mama bear wilderness on her face. No one moved to intervene on Dune's imminent ass-whupping.

After a moment's breath, the woman stepped back, positioning herself between Dune and the boy. Dune noticed that the woman didn't touch the boy. Mama had the same massive eyes as her son, hers red rimmed and swollen, dangerously alert. She was compact and round, wearing a sweatshirt several sizes too big for her, the sleeves cut off at her elbows, her hair a soft unkempt haze around her face escaping a brown scarf, gathered in lumpy puffs under the satin.

"Where'd he get sick?" Dune asked gently, as if the woman had just strolled up easily.

"What? The fuck? You a doctor?" The woman deserved a person to be angry at. She was watching her child die, slowly, for no apparent reason. Dune stood still, a cloud being passed through by the sharp edges of a winged creature. The woman looked at Dune's eyes, darting back and forth, right and left. "At the house! Why?"

"They seem to do a little better if you keep them near the place they got sick," Dune offered, gentle, her eyes hawking the boy.

Since Red, Dune had taken to moving people inside their home if she found them outside, laying them down if she found them standing, increasing the comfort of transition, in lieu of curing them, in absence of magic.

Dune didn't know why advice was the first thing she offered up, immediately regretted it. The boy was so lovely, how was it possible that he couldn't come back?

Mama Bear turned away from Dune, just shook her head. "Better? Tuh. No one gets fucking better." Her breath was slowing down, the words she spoke seemed to hurt her. "His daddy gone, his brother gone. I can't do it again."

Mama Bear was lost in her own suffering, standing next to her son, following his lost gaze out the window. Dune faced the maze of empty fountains with them for a moment. She was surprised this mama hadn't gone too, all that loss on her face.

"I could give you my address if it would help." Dune felt the seed of an idea forming as she said this aloud. The woman looked raw for a moment, considering. "If you need to leave … I'm staying."

"I'm not leaving my baby." Mama sounded disgusted.

Dune understood what was out beyond the woman's words, the exhaustion of grieving so continuously, for so many. She shrugged a little at Mama Bear and thought to the boy, looking at his perfect young baby boy face, "*get free.*"

She slipped back down the stairs, feeling the attention of the atrium shifting away from the edge of conflict, eyes on her drifting back to their own business. She found her reluctant placeholder and eased back into the line. People were trading stories, numbers, theories about the sick, the wasting away, the dead. One person repeated the rumor that if sick people came in with generational insurance, they got hooked up to life support machines, dropped into induced comas to stop the flood of tears, a controlled wall of silence.

Dune didn't like the idea of taking away the small whispered communication—who knew how hard it was for the grievers to get those words out?

Her Reluctant Placeholder, when folks in the line started to get excited by this gossiped possibility, snapped that those machines were all occupied. "We can't convince no one to loan us anything with no end in sight," she added. "Just delaying the inevitable anyway, what's the point?"

"I just want to opt out of the incinerator cremation!" A man responded. Dune felt shocked—certainly hospitals, morgues, had cremation options? But others seemed to accept that bodies were going through the incinerator.

"That's only for the homeless though."

"Anyone can look homeless real quick if they get sick alone in the street."

"Shit some of us was homeless 'til everyone left." This from a woman whose face seemed permanently frozen in a surprised smile. There were some chuckles, some glances of suspicion. "What they suppose to do?"

This was really the most dreadful part of a crisis at this scale: what to do with the too-many bodies? Kama, this boy, they had loved ones to let them go. There were thousands of others whose stories weren't getting told, whose names were unknown, whose pictures never made the cover of anything. They became numbers, erased twice.

Dune didn't repeat her mistake of volunteering advice or even theories. She listened. She learned more waiting in that line than she'd gotten out of the radio.

The half of the city that had still been employed when the plague came had finally given up the farce of all but essential health and emergency response jobs. Child Protective Services was evacuating all healthy kids they found, even if their parents didn't want to leave. It was unclear where they were taking the kids. Those not doing official emergency response work were mostly taking care of family, neighbors or strangers in their homes, hiding their children, or spending time at these centers, seeking answers that didn't exist.

They were all her, she was all of them.

As the line doubled back on itself, Dune found herself passing the women who looked like farmers. They were quiet, but she felt their attention; felt familiar, but not known. She caught the eye of one woman, who nodded at her.

"Are you on your own?" The woman asked. She was older, slender, her hands large, folded together in front of her. The other two seemed to rock away from the one who asked the question.

Dune was cautious. "No."

The woman nodded, a smirk at her eyes, Dune thought maybe this stranger approved of her reticence. "We're trying to find chickens. You know of any?"

Dune wished she knew of a chicken. She desperately missed eggs, that had been one of the first things to disappear from the stores. Sometimes the food bags had the liquid egg mix in a box, but Dune didn't trust that stuff. She shook her head.

"Well, we come here every week, about this time. If you hear of any chickens." The woman turned away a bit, closing the conversation. Dune felt like she had missed something, some brief window flashed open with sun beyond it that she only clocked as it swung shut. She peeked at the trio when she could. One of the women was tall and thick through the chest and mid-section, lighter skinned. The third was actually quite glamorous upon closer reflection. Her nails were short, but bright red, and her eyebrows were so perfect that Dune wondered if they were drawn on.

Dune was left with a yawning loneliness. She wanted a we, some company, peers, comrades. She wanted a squad to survive the apocalypse with.

By the time Dune got to the front of the line it had been five hours of waiting, inching around the atrium. The line concluded at several wooden tables on metal legs in front of an open door to a room full of bags and supplies. There was a row of people behind the tables, with volunteers in matching orange shirts running back and forth from the table to the back room.

Dune stepped forward to the blonde woman behind the table, who was wearing a white face mask over the bottom of her face under green eyes that were tiny, dull and never rested on anything for longer than a second. She introduced herself with a name Dune immediately forgot. She was automatically handing Dune a grocery bag full of what appeared to be spaghetti noodles, cans of tomato sauce and tuna fish.

When Dune didn't move, the lady said with light annoyance, "What else can I do for you?" Dune decided to call her Jen. Dune could tell that maybe Jen had been a perky helper type once, but upon cursory inspection, Jen looked absolutely exhausted, shadows carved down the visible surface of her face, hair limp and pulled back, and just a flat glaze in those small busy eyes.

"I was wondering if you have any updated information on taking care of the sick."

Jen didn't say anything for a moment, just stared at Dune. When she finally spoke, her tone held no curiosity. "Sorry, what do you mean? You got bodies?"

Dune shook her head. "No. Yeah, I just mean ... the sick people. They're everywhere."

"Are these people members of your family?" Jen looked marginally incredulous.

"No. Most of my family is dead."

Jen nodded, normalizing the sentence without offering any pity. Dune expected nothing more. Even before H-8 no one knew what to do about death. "These are other people that I have found around. I'm not asking about curing them, I understand that that isn't possible at this time, or we would have heard about it."

Jen didn't nod or confirm this and Dune realized that some part of her had hoped Jen would interrupt and say, "Actually they found a miraculous cure just this morning that's being bottled and distributed right over this table."

Dune continued, "I am just wondering if there are any tips on getting folks to drink water or ... just anything to help make it easier."

Jen shook her head. "No. Not that we know of. Life support doesn't even seem to be a particularly helpful thing at this point. Just my opinion. These folks are dead as soon as they get sick. I think maybe it's kinder to let it be quicker. So just keep calling the crisis line, 611."

Dune was the quiet one now. She felt a pressure in her chest, tight in a way she couldn't place.

"You from here?" she asked Jen.

"No. Virginia. Came up to volunteer. But—"

"Have you lost anyone to H-8?"

Dune could sense Jen's lips tighten behind the face mask as the volunteer realized she was under attack. "I've been here for a month, working nonstop. And thousands of patients have come through these crisis centers. Thousands. Prolonging those deaths didn't help."

Dune felt her face burn, trying to contain something inappropriate.

"Y'all don't know what it is. Good, 'kind' deaths isn't the point. Staying alive so that maybe someone finds a cure and we can save our lives, that is the point." Dune's voice felt quiet, like it was shrinking in on itself to get through her throat.

Jen shrugged now, her head twisting away dismissively. "Well. I hope that works, I hope for a cure too."

Dune realized that she needed to get out of this woman's presence. She wanted to reach across the table and grab Jen's neck, just under the blonde hairline, and start shaking her head and body in different directions.

It wasn't Jen's fault, what she was saying. She was expressing something Dune had heard before.

Let the dying die, let the dead go.

"I *am* sorry," Jen said, leaning forward, rearranging her stapler, her tone final—an invitation to leave. It was hard to rely on only a stranger's eyes for information. "About your family. And I am *not* trying to be insensitive. But you need to leave these sick people alone and stay in your house. They're going to evacuate y'all soon. The best thing *you* can do right now is live."

Dune's eyes went sharp with tears that came on so fast they hurt. She was not willing to cry here. "I'm not fucking leaving!

Everyone I know and love is here, they live on this stinking fuck ass wind. You don't know what you're even saying. Live!? What the fuck kind of life are we supposed to live!? We're all alone here, Jen!! With a bunch of people who are sick and won't stop crying and won't even drink fucking water and you think I should just leave them out in the cold and let them freeze to death or bring them here to die in your 611 back room? I don't care what *you* would do, you're a visitor moving numbers! You leave here and go back to some place where the people you love are safe, and warm, and talking to you. Shit, *you* should just fucking leave. *You* should just go, so those of us here can figure out how to stop this shit. I didn't come in here for your fucking life coaching. I just want to know one thing and if you don't know the answer, Jen? If you don't have a fucking clue? Then just say that and I will figure it out my goddamn motherfucking self!"

Dune was as loud as she had ever been, spit flying across the table. The whole crisis center was quiet. She was suddenly that person. She had never been that person before. She was breathing hard, tears streaming down her face. Jen looked like a kicked dog.

"My name is Sarah," Jen said, not quite meeting Dune's eyes.

Dune held the tension in her body for a moment and then it broke, and she started chuckling, and then laughing so hard her head fell back. Jen/Sarah's eyes looked even more concerned. From within, Dune was watching herself lose her mind. She was in a crazy city full of—or more accurately, empty with—crazy people. Crazy people dying quietly, crazy people helping when no help was actually useful. Who cared what anyone thought of her anymore? She was thirsty on behalf of people who no longer remembered they could drink water.

"Come on now honey," a voice spoke. Reluctant Placeholder

was standing next to her, she'd been talking to another volunteer. She placed a hand on Dune's back and pointed towards the door with her head and then turned and walked away.

"Right." Bitter tongue, bitter voice. "Sarah. Nice to meet you, Sarah. Ok. Thanks for the food, Sarah." Dune picked up the bag aggressively and stepped back from the table. Her heart was beating on the outer edges of her body. She needed to get out of this building. She turned and saw the people, Mama Bear, the farmers, the humans full of gossip and composure.

She stood up taller and strutted past all the people, trying not to make eye contact. Or she tucked her head in and slipped away.

She couldn't tell what her body was doing anymore.

chapter seventeen

Wage Love

Mama Vivian had listened to the news, each morning of her adult life, even while she labored with Brendon, even in the sunrise hours after Wes's death. Each day, Dune asked Mama Vivian if she wanted to hear some news on her little antenna radio.

Today, as was often the case, the only response was a fleeting eye contact, Mama's face still tilted towards the window. As much a yes as anything else. Dune inserted her grandmother's hearing aids, turned them all the way up, then turned on WDET.

"Tuning in to the live press conference from Atlanta, with Sally Burns, Center for Disease Control's expert on Syndrome H-8."

Dune laughed, everything was terror or entertainment in a free fall. An expert on H-8? In Atlanta?

Now a voice that sounded anxious and authoritative. "And please don't put even more people at risk by taking this disease beyond the barriers of Detroit! So far the majority of cases have been identified within the 8-Mile inner city radius and we want to keep it that way. But it depends on you, on all of us. Please keep yourself and your sick hydrated. If you are not sick, we want to keep you that way! Listen for the food shuttles passing through your area."

There was some shuffling sound and then the host's voice came back on the radio. "Well. There you have it, Jim. Stay put, stay hydrated and get some free food."

Dune's mouth twisted her nose sideways and she peeked at Mama Vivian, whose lips were pursed, possibly also annoyed. Dune said, "No one's staying here Mama. They're just saying that to cover their asses. If it's contagious like that, it's out there."

Mama Vivian held Dune's gaze, which felt like encouragement. Dune shook her head, showing her judgment. "Stay hydrated. But it might be in the water. Stay in Detroit. It's contagious there."

Mama Vivian almost seemed to smile, a softening around the mouth. Dune couldn't remember what her grandmother sounded like. She played with the knobs on the radio, turning to WWJ.

"This is unacceptable!" Dune knew that voice. She tried to turn it up, but it was as high as it could go. "The Sick already overwhelmed the hospitals, the crisis centers, I mean, there's not life support equipment like that in the city! The mayor's wife is on life support. Half the Pistons and Tigers are on life support. That's it! What about us? Even with other places sending they machines— got Amtrak full of defibrillators. But people who don't have healthcare aren't even eligible for the life support options. And we're supposed to be grateful they just now quarantining us? And they only quarantining us now because Alice de Costa is sick. No offense to the mayor, I don't diminish her grief in anyway. I am so sorry her wife is sick, I truly am. But it's like—now you believe in it? Now? No! No quarantine, who does that protect at this point? If this was New York or LA they would have quarantined us in

July and who knows, maybe it could have been contained. Too late. Shit, if this was happening in Kenya they would have stopped allowing Kenyans to travel to this whole *country* at all the very first day. Emergency management? Man, y'all don't know what it is, or how it's spread, and you've just let everyone go everywhere. And no one, not one person who has gotten sick, has recovered. We are dying in here! We overwhelmed the morgues too! We need a cure. Everyone's going to need a cure.

"Somebody needs to help us, this is a total crisis!"

A host came on, voice like a fire pit. "With us in the studio this morning, community activist Elouise Knight. Mrs. Knight, what kind of help can people give? What can normal Detroiters do about this crisis?"

"For one thing we need to believe us. People seem to think we been making this whole thing up—I honestly can't believe the National Guard is just now being called in—and I don't even want some military solution but at least that is a step of taking this seriously. We need our water tested. We need our air tested. We need data on where people are getting sick, and when. Stop the misinformation! It's only Black people getting sick. We know! People need information. We are holding a meeting tomorrow at the St. Regis, 3pm, to talk about this National Guard stuff, and all of this. If you are well, you need to come through. We are fighting for this city's soul right now, we really are!"

Dune's eyes crept over to Mama Vivian with guilt or, more precisely, a desire to be absolved of guilt.

Elouise was a dear family friend. Kama and Brendon would have been at that meeting—they probably would have organized it. Or Mama Vivian would have, once, guiding everyone to look for collective solutions. And Dune was just here in the house, or driving around chasing sick people, only thinking of her remaining tiny family, her questions, doing her research all alone.

Mama Vivian gave her no respite, no attention at all. Her old eyes were closed, but flicking open every few minutes as if she was nervous to surrender to sleep. Dune leaned forward and kissed Mama Vivian on the forehead then, feeling judged and a bit resentful. She left the room to go lay in her mother's bed.

....

"This is an outrage!"

A flurry of motherland cloth moved around the midnight black force called Elouise Knight, six feet tall, broad as an oak. She was battling from the front of the ballroom of the St. Regis, "You don't know what it is making us sick! You don't know how to make us better. But *you* are going to mandate that we stay here? That's genocide!"

Dune just barely stepped into the room and slipped left, hanging against the back wall. It felt like the AC was still blowing in the room, even though it was cold outside.

The meeting was packed full of leftover Detroiters, strangers mostly, but a few familiar faces. People were looking for some clarity, some answers. Human bundles in late fall layers were spread around the shabby room on stackable golden chairs with soft brown pleather seats. There was no order to the arrangement of bodies, no real front or focal point—no one wanted to be here.

After what the city now acknowledged was months of a growing crisis, the National Guard had shown up two days earlier with no warning or explanation. This response meeting had been called with radio and flyers, to discuss the presence of the National Guard and the future. Dune was amazed at how full the room was. There are people who listen to the radio, who respond to flyers; Dune had grown up going to meetings full of passionate, suspicious luddites. But that, too, was changing as the conspiracies manifested. This was a cross section of organizers, artists, journalists and entrepreneurs. Equalized by H-8.

There were no allies, no advocates. Each civilian there was on the front line, had witnessed the sickness, been untrained hospice and sometimes gravedigger for their loved ones. They wanted answers. They needed to hear a compelling future.

Standing out like a hand made of thumbs, a row of National Guard soldiers sat together near the front of the room. They'd lined up their chairs straight amidst the chaos, except for one soldier, Black and stocky, leaning back in his chair, arms crossed.

The room was not united.

A smallish white man in black spectacles was speaking, "We don't know what it is, how it's spread. What if we carry it with us, if it's in us? What if we infect other places?" He had a long bright red beard, dark green eyes. Dune knew his face, even his work, but couldn't bring to mind his name. "We don't know enough about it. We don't know the incubation period. We don't know if it's like typhoid, with carriers who don't get sick themselves. It is absolutely a tragedy what is happening here—and we don't want to compound that tragedy by unknowingly spreading the disease to other places."

Elouise turned to face him, arms spread wide like wings, as if preparing to dive bomb into his soft belly. "What if we don't, Matt? What if this violent act of imprisoning us in a place where we *know* people are dying just leads to the death of the majority of this city? This Black city! Because guess what, I love you, but other than you most of the white folk left immediately! Indian Village? Empty. Boston-Edison? Empty. Midtown? Empty! The Westin is empty! Did they infect New York, LA, Martha's Vineyard, wherever the heck they went? No! It's just us, in here, in the only place we *know for sure* we can get sick!"

Several people in the room clapped at Elouise's words, Black and Brown hands solid against each other, faces stern and stubborn. Even though they lacked the power to stop the syndrome, it was galvanizing to feel right.

"And don't think we can't see that it's activists disproportionately getting sick, people who have been here and fought and bled for this city. We in this room are about all that's left of the movement folk. That's an accident? No! Let us out of here!"

There had been so many ways the city was abandoned before this. Many of the people in the room were the reason there was still a Detroit worth its salt. There was Rhodesia Clarke, who had been heading up Black efforts for climate justice throughout the city; Hoka Watkins, a racial justice educator and adversary-comrade of Mama Vivian's. The women over sixty were all Mama something unless they were queer or white.

As a teenager Dune had worked alongside Elouise for years, volunteering on water rights campaigns under Kama's wing. Dune trusted Elouise's judgment, and felt moved by her presence.

Elouise was an auntie to Dune and many others. She had been part of Kama's support circle after Brendon died, bringing food and talking about the accident and the man as long as Kama needed, when other people were scared to broach the topic. The two women could fill an evening with venting, fill a room with rage. Now it fed Dune to see such unchecked passion, even if it felt a mile away from her own heart.

Dune had no interest in leaving Detroit. Where would she go? All she wanted was to understand why her mother was gone.

"Ma'am. Sergeant Miles Booker." One of the young guardsmen

stood up and spoke with his chin thrust up, holding his hat in some sort of deference to the crowd. His whiteness was a glaring part of his look. Most of the men in uniform Dune could see were white. Either no one had thought about the optics, or the Guard knew what everyone in Detroit suspected: that white bodies were safe from the syndrome. "No one is imprisoning anyone. Everyone here is free to stay ... in their own home." The crowd groaned. "Anywhere within the epicenter of the crisis you can move about freely. Unfortunately, we don't have the luxury of only thinking about the 504,000 people in Detroit. We have to think about the 324 million people currently living within these borders, whom we protect. Now, of course, that includes y'all—"

"Don't lie!" Elouise's body snapped, her voice filling the room in a way that left no air for nonsense. "Don't lie to us! We not in some luxurious delusion! Just subtract us then. If we are the expendable enemy you contain? There is not one shred of evidence that this plague is spread between people. It comes over people who have never met, in isolation. But it comes here! In this place! If you put a wall around Detroit, you are locking us in a room with a rabid dog! And you won't even admit it?"

Elouise spun around then, a warrior dancer in a frenzy, and faced the crowd. Dune couldn't look away. She noticed the sullen guardsman, still sitting back, swarthy, with a sour set to his chin. He caught Dune's eye, shrugged with one shoulder. Dune softly sucked her teeth at him and grabbed her elbows, turning away.

"I am not going out like this!" Elouise's eyes flashed over Dune and she lifted her arms to the room as if she wanted to gather all of them into her heart. "We have an ancestral responsibility to this place, to each other, to beat this, to survive! As Mama Kama taught us, 'to live and not die!'"[3]

Dune felt a sting, hearing her mother's name out loud. Others in the room shifted, giving her, Kama's grieving daughter, their attention. Dune felt the weight of her blood. She remembered something that had slipped away in her months of private grief: her mother had been a powerful teacher in the movement. Now she was a convincing reference.

Dune was ashamed amongst these people. She had tuned out her mother's precious last words until recently, and she didn't know how to insert the directive, "wage love," how to explain the kind of fight her mother was calling for. She hadn't considered any of these people, this beloved community, in Kama's dying, in her death. Hadn't allowed them to honor her. Kama had only been hers.

She waited until the crowd returned their attention to Elouise, slipping out the door as they all started to take to their feet with shouts of affirmation.

She agreed with everyone about Detroit. They should leave, they should stay. They should quarantine, they should evacuate. It all seemed viable in this new world. She didn't want to see this horrible death spread to any other places.

She agreed with Elouise in theory, somehow it was the city itself that was sick, both source and victim of this endless loss. She just didn't have somewhere else she wanted to be. She couldn't imagine leaving the cocoon of mother-grief, the house where her memories were shaped, the streets where her parents loved her out loud.

The hallway of the old hotel had unreasonably high ceilings dripping with chandeliers, meant to give a grand impression to bustling, important guests. Mama Vivian had told her many times the story of staying at the St. Regis the first time she visited the city in 1967, feeling glamorous, piling her small luggage on a velvet lined cart.

Today the decaying glamour was unsettling, a dry Titanic. The walls were papered in a way that had once been fashionable, and now looked faded, printed dappled gourds with grapes pouring out, one after another, in a diagonal pattern as far as the eye cared to look.

Dune slunk out between art deco doors thick with glass panes. She looked in both directions. The early fall day was gray, cool, damp. The hard cold was still about a month out.

Dune blurred her gaze until she could see through the present, her time traveling eyes laying a city onto the city. Her soft gaze saw lanky Black boy bodies with faded faux-hawks or tiny loc starters, on bikes whose spokes strobed the sunlight as they turned fast off of Grand and pumped north on Second. Young girls full of chicken and waffles from New Center Eatery, holding hands, a rainbow of barrettes in newly plaited hair under trees brash with tangerine and beet-colored leaves on the branches.

Not this year.

When her eyes sharpened to the present moment again, there was no one in sight. The sun was pushing the rain off, but couldn't seem quite able to find true yellow, such that the light and the clusters of buildings in it looked nauseous.

Dune slipped a silver cigarette case out of her back pocket and pulled out a spliff. She rolled her own magic cigarettes, dusting a generous pinch of weed over her tobacco. The one purchase she'd made with Paulie's guilt money was a few pounds of potent shake from Joe, the white boy who had run a dispensary over on Gratiot. Neither of them commented on the massive purchase, both knowing she was stocking up in case he got sick before she could visit again.

She was even saving the seeds. Just in case.

She propped the sole of her left foot against the brick wall behind her and let the weight drop back in her hips, adjusting where her jeans were pulling tighter than she expected. She didn't want to fill out her pants, spill belly over the tight waist. She didn't want any part of the burden of being a body, lugging herself around, betraying her mother with each breath.

When her spliff had disappeared into fire and a spacious calm in her belly, Dune closed her eyes and let the quiet fill her up, let the solid weight of the wall hold her.

chapter eighteen

Grievers

Dune felt the first town hall participant coming down the hall through the glass, movement in her periphery. She stepped further away from the entrance.

The door burst open and the guardsmen stepped out, heads bowed, walking quickly to their van parked in the guest drop-off zone across a threadbare red carpet.

Dune considered taking one of the rolling golden luggage racks as her skateboard home. She tried to imagine it, pushing herself down Woodward, flying, the luggage rack a paper airplane, her as the aerodynamic nose. She couldn't bring the ground into her vision, even with effort.

Soon the whole room was streaming by, a river of survivors respecting her downturned eyes. Elouise stepped out of the doors last, holding a roll of paper in one hand, two massive purses balancing her wide shoulders, her sensible nurse shoes at odds with her bright dress, a cape somehow over and under it all. She saw Dune and set down her load.

A massive smile started at the horizon of Elouise's upper lip and sunrose up her face, only the faintest grief pulling the outer edges of her full lips back down. The gap in her teeth was radiant. Dune found a big smile reflecting from her own mouth before she knew it. Elouise reached her arms out first and pulled Dune into the amber scented pillow of her breasts.

"Baby girl, I am so, so sorry about your mama."

With no warning, Dune was crying hard. In public. For the first time. This wasn't done, she knew, but she couldn't help herself. Elouise, her body soft and strong like Kama's, seemed like she could take it all on.

And Elouise met the emotion with her own as she wept with Dune.

She murmured into Dune's hair, "No one as brave, no one who held her line as tough. She was so good. So good, honey, so good."

Elouise held Dune for a long time, grief crashing back and forth between their hearts.

"Great job in there," Dune spoke finally, pulling back and wiping her face with her t-shirt as her breath started to land.

"I don't understand how they think they can just make decisions like that with no warning!" Elouise's eyes were hard for a moment. Then her age lines gave way to softness and she shrugged at Dune, shaking her head. "It's no use. I'd be mad if they were forcing us to leave too. It's an impossible place. It's not that many of us left. They have to include us in this process."

"Yeah. I guess just ... who? You know?"

"Girl I do not know. Everyday I wake up and cannot believe I am still here." Elouise slid down the glass until the ground caught her, sat still. Dune slipped down and leaned her head on Elouise's shoulder.

Neither of them had been very physical with their affection in the years they had known each other, worked together. Dune wondered why not, it felt so comfortable.

Elouise turned her face into Dune's unkempt hair, "How are you?"

Dune answered without moving, "I'm here."

"You eating enough? Sleeping right?"

"I'm eating too much honestly." At this Dune grabbed a handful of her softening belly, handling it as if it belonged to another person. "Can't stop. And having crazy dreams!"

"First of all, no such thing as too much in a body surviving trauma. Chile, when my mother died, I changed shape. And I began to do work in my dreams. Crazy just means honest sometimes. Write them down if you can, consider it another realm of ideas and growth."

Dune accepted this homework, with doubts. She often woke up with the imprints of dreams all over her mind and body, her sheets in the disarray of an active sleeper. But she rarely kept hold of any memories, any details.

"What about Mama Vivian?" Elouise was patient with her questions, pulling Dune into conversation step by step.

"She's confused. I think she wants to die."

Even now Dune felt too far from Mama Vivian, sitting here. She was never sure if her grandmother actually understood her when she said where she was going, how long she'd be gone. The wandering eyes that punctuated Mama Vivian's time seemed to be looking for her across the city miles now. Elouise nodded as if wanting to die was the most logical response to this moment.

Dune asked, "What about you?"

"Oh fine. Fine. Lou wants to go while we still can."

When Elouise spoke of her husband, she always smiled as if he amused her, especially when she spoke of their disagreements. Dune doubted Big Lou had won a single argument in their entire relationship and suspected that was why the marriage worked. Elouise gestured around her, adding, "Most everyone else already left. But I'm not leaving until everyone can."

Dune nodded. She expected no less from Elouise, although she couldn't say what kind of justice it would be to abandon the city en masse, vs staying and dying.

Elouise leaned back to look at Dune's face as she asked, "You staying too?"

Dune shrugged with her mouth. "I've been gathering stories." As the words were coming out she didn't know how to explain what she was doing down in the basement. Research? Building a model cemetery? Some sacred unspeakable ritual? She visualized the notes and images she had started placing in columns on the wall, the scaled-up model of the city, the maps.

Yes, among other possible things, these were stories, gathered.

"That is so necessary! How else we going to learn about this epidemic if we don't really study it?" Elouise was so earnest in her responses, so authentic that it made Dune feel something flutter in her through the fog.

They were not dead. She was here with her beloved auntie Elouise, who wasn't berating her for how she had been in her grief, who always seemed to dance as she spoke, moving the hundred beaded necklaces around her neck into a rocking motion, hands shaping and reshaping the air.

"Who are you interviewing?"

Dune sucked the inside of her lower lip. Admitting this might mark her for madness. "I am listening to people who get sick."

Elouise's face gathered up in a question and she lifted herself from the wall and turned towards Dune, as if this was too large a thing to say side by side. Dune felt the cool air where they'd been touching. Elouise grabbed Dune's small shoulders in her big working hands, searching the girl's face for miracles. "They *talk* to you? You can *talk* to them?"

Dune shook her head. "I don't think they hear me. I just grab the words they're saying."

Elouise let her go, confusion twisting her face. Dune feltazed by how wide the range of Elouise's expressions were, each one full volume. "What you mean?"

"For the first week or so, when people first get sick." Dune realized there wasn't really a language for this crisis yet, other than time and death. "They are almost always saying, whispering, something."

"Yes, the mouths!" Elouise was a lightbulb coming on a rickety fuse, flashing to brightness. "I thought it was just babbling."

"It is. Sometimes there's words. I document that. Basically, where they are when they get sick, and what they are saying, if it's clear. And ... anything else."

"Wow! Like clues? Wow. What a way of honoring our people! We should all be doing that!" Elouise grew taller with the thought.

It hadn't occurred to Dune to get others to join her. Elouise turned towards the door as if she wanted to go back in and recruit right now. "That should be the next town hall, 'Listening to Our Sick!' 'Black Voices from Beyond!' We can map the area out and try to at least get everyone who is infected now. Shame is, I've been so scared of them, scared of my own! I didn't even—we could come see who you've documented so far. This will give us something to do 'til they let us out of here or figure out what's wrong."

Dune felt a little thrill in her belly. It was a familiar feeling, when it seems like the world can be changed by some action that happens at the scale of a few committed people. She was raised attuned to this feeling of possibility, could trace it throughout the years, flowing through her mother, flowing through a crowd at the downtown Detroit rallies on water ownership or food deserts or impossible heating bills or other human rights concerns, during the big marches on Washington she had attended as a teenager, walking between Brendon and Kama and feeling connected to everything alive.

She mostly didn't trust the feeling anymore, after years of having it followed swiftly by some reminder of who held power and who didn't.

Kama had always told her the feeling wasn't about anything that could be put on paper, it was the feeling of being of this earth. "You are a child of mother earth and sometimes you can feel the connection as undeniable," she'd say.

Dune felt a cellular battle between her cynicism and her hope, who she came from versus who she was. In this moment, she let it all shiver, let Elouise's desperate hope infect her.

"You don't think people would be too scared?"

"I mean, *most* of us are not hiding in a bunker, we out here." Elouise twisted her mouth at this in a way that made Dune wonder who was hiding in a bunker. And was it working? "Might as well be doing something meaningful."

Dune nodded.

"I'll go with you," Elouise spoke to the doubt on Dune's face. Her mother had been the one who could normally do that, read her, respond to the unspoken in her. "I'll do it for a week and if that works then we can invite others."

Elouise sounded excited inside the risk and Dune understood it. Purpose yielded bravery, or at least reframed survival.

"Ok," Dune said. "Come by tomorrow, I'll show you what I have so far."

The women hugged each other close. Elouise loaded her bags and papers into the vegetable crate strapped on the back of her bike with bungie cord. As she mounted the wide seat, Dune thought she looked like a Black Gilda, a good witch, skin shimmering with sensible magic.

Elouise biked east down the middle of the road, looking neither left nor right as she crossed Woodward.

Dune started the isolated walk home along Grand, glad she had chosen to use her feet today, move a little slower. She wanted to move slow enough to keep this little flame lit in her heart.

She'd been so lost in her grief, getting through the days, seeing only the sick people—she hadn't tracked the emptying of the city, the closing up of businesses. When had the St. Regis closed to guests? Of course, who was coming to visit this place anyway? She could feel the absence of life here, but felt like she had blinked and missed the actual change happening. Now the city was becoming the apocalyptic wasteland others had projected onto it for years through their selective reporting and photography.

She could see almost all the way to the river, so many boarded windows beneath black and gray buildings, no buses running, no light rail. Just the wide road, cut for Cadillacs, Packard Clippers and Model-Ts.

Woodward was a mixture of buildings abandoned both for a long time and quite recently. The difference showed in the age of the wood over the windows, the amount of graffiti, the state of the signs above the doors.

People had called Detroit a crisis most of her life, disaster capitalists indulging in ruin porn, finding beauty in the disintegration of the city's dreams. Dune knew the way it looked when only every other building was boarded up, the ones in between teeming with life, women praising Jesus, cursing Republicans while getting their hair done. She missed old men walking into soul food spots that doubled as bars in the evenings, walking out with plastic bags tied tightly around styrofoam containers brimming with fried catfish sandwiches, crusty mac and cheese, collard greens and packets of tartar and hot sauce. She missed live music everywhere. She even missed frustrated lines out the door of the precinct up ahead of her, Black faces with fierce eyes ready to battle bureaucracy.

She missed the vibrant half city she'd known and taken for granted.

She passed her barber shop, which had no boards, just a chain on the security gate. Part of her queer life had been coming here to have the shaved sides of her head lined up. She appreciated getting to be a quiet witness to the conversations men had while they waited to be clipped and shaved—it was different from the salons. The men spoke in sentences that didn't necessarily build off each other's content, but off the disgruntled feelings about the content, the prices of things, gas, mechanics, games at the big stadiums. They raged against change and told awestruck stories of their powerful and manipulative wives.

Taking in the empty chairs, unused tools, the dark face of the television, Dune missed the narrative life of that little room. She hoped everyone had made it out.

Soon she was walking under the railway tracks by the Amtrak station. Since the Guard had arrived a couple days ago, trains had been whistling in, pallets of food landing, unloaded systematically, distributed in open bed camouflage trucks heading out to the sub-urbs and border, places that still had people lining up for help. A train sat on the tracks now.

Dune looked up—the tree-line looked like blown glass, gold and rouge. And there, the wounded sky was visible between the two bridges that carried life east and west. She saw several people in the windows of the train's cabin. They wore what looked like a pale green uniform, structured. They seemed to be watching her, but they all had on gas masks, so she couldn't tell for sure. They never left the train.

The soldiers crawling on and over the train wore white face masks and gloves, every other inch of skin covered in a dark forest pattern. Their warrior layers looked claustrophobic to Dune. The invisible enemy, the unknown foe, was it floating in the air? Was it on saliva or etched onto the buildings themselves in a code that rewrote the body's desires?

Dune wondered if she looked as ridiculous to them as they did to her, her face exposed, her hands bare in her pockets, available to the sickness in ways they thought they were not.

Go go go, she thought at them. Life is not here.

....

The two men fit the exact same description.

Dune was going through her basement records, wanting every-thing current before she showed Elouise.

One sick man had been on Woodward, the other on Mack just around the corner. They both wore jeans and black shirts with small company logos on them, sneakers. One of them had words—"rig, dollop, sansa?" The other had none. She'd made little cards for them and printed images, but the quality of photo between her crappy phone and the ancient printer wouldn't help loved ones make the distinction. Her system wasn't good enough.

If the one with words, if his family was looking through her data for him, they wouldn't know for sure if it was this blurry shadow or the other guy. She needed more distinction.

Dune went through Brendon's office boxes in the basement corner, looking for something she slightly remembered him having—a polaroid camera. Or it might have just been a normal camera distinct from a phone? Either way it was something old and higher quality, but she couldn't quite remember which and she couldn't find it.

She went upstairs and opened Kama's closet, scanning the boxes stacked up the left side. There were three boxes of Brendon's things that Kama liked to have close by. Dune touched her fingers to the top box, the cardboard abused, mended at the corners with duct tape. She had a fleeting sense of kinship with these boxes, leftover and full, carrying priceless forgettable objects from other lives.

Something made her pause in her pawing at the boxes.

She turned away from the closet and looked at the bone bed, framed by ashes. Light was pouring in the room strangely again, a horizontal line across the top half of the bed, the vases of mother ash shining.

Take Kama downstairs. This idea occurred to her as if spoken by another. But within the walls of her mind. She listened for another moment, waited. Was that her own thought?

She shook her head, but crossed the creaky bedroom floor and squatted next to the vase on the left side of the bed. She touched it gently and then slid down against it, hugging it, feeling it still part of her mother's sick body.

As she stood up, she hitched the vase full of Kama against her body and carried it down the hall. Slowly, stepping backwards and resting the vase on the step above her when she needed to, she got it downstairs to the basement. Then she went and got the other vase, leaving the bones hidden on her mother's pillow. On the second trip, she paused at the altar and stuffed the envelope of money from Paulie Vereen under her shirt.

In the basement, she slowly pushed the vases under the card tables, into the middle, until, standing, she could barely see them. On an instinct, she got on her knees and half crawled, half scooted herself under. She pulled the tops off the vases, letting Kama breathe.

"That's the last time I carry you," she grunted, backing out from under the tables, clapping her hands clean while catching her breath.

Standing up, she felt the edge of the envelope against her rib. She pulled it into the basement light. This man had killed her father. And he knew it. She couldn't imagine living with that. She pulled out a handful of the cash that she couldn't imagine really using. She set the envelope amongst the other supplies on the shelf and spent some time stuffing cash under the vases to lift them closer to the underside of the table.

Kama and Brendon were together. That felt right. Everything, anything was allowed by her loss. She couldn't say why, not to any judge or jury. But having done this, she exhaled.

Dune went back up to Kama's room, which felt brighter, clearer now. She opened the top box in the closet. Right on top were three cameras, each in its own Ziploc freezer bag—a Polaroid with no film, a fancy black masterpiece with an assortment of detached lenses, and a small digital handheld wrapped with its cord. She blessed her father's Virgo tendencies and took the digital one from the box.

She closed the box up. That was enough touching her grief for one night.

....

"Oh Dune—it's an altar!"

Elouise stood next to the model, hands resting on her round belly. Dune felt competing emotions at this new experience of having another human standing down here—she felt protective over what she had created, proud of the detail and care.

Dune showed Elouise each of the systems, everything she had so far. The little signs for each person she had found. The cards, organized alphabetically by neighborhood. The images. Elouise wanted to understand each one.

After reviewing it all, looking at it from every angle, Elouise repeated herself. "It's sacred work, love. It's an altar."

Dune hesitated to own that. "I've been seeing it as a research project. I mean Kama used to make altars. But we never had some clear lineage. I don't want to be ..." Dune paused, then made a gesture of grabbing things all around her.

"You can't. Don't worry."

"Yes, I can. I don't belong to anything, it doesn't belong to me."

"Well that's just the thing," Elouise turned to Dune with soft eyes. "When everything has been taken, filling that emptiness ain't appropriation. It's something else. It ain't pure, none of it. I think of these practices, my Orisha, my altars, my prayers and chants, and all this accumulation of spiritual armor, as something to comfort me when my ancestral ghost limbs hurt. Because I need Spirit so much! I answer what calls me—Spirit is bigger than any one lineage! It comes through all these channels. It's complicated, beautifully complicated. But it ain't appropriation, not amongst displaced and denied peoples. It's different."

Dune was quiet, accepting the permission Elouise offered, letting the moment of divine tremble up an energy between them.

"I mean, at minimum, it's sacred data." Elouise lifted a brow at Dune and moved in closer to the east side. Dune saw the moment Elouise noticed the mold. It didn't look like the artificial squares of grass. It looked fungal and buoyant, and it was all over the model, not universal, not chaotic, but in every neighborhood with territorial precision. Dune could not think of any explanation for it, or for why she'd given up trying to wipe it away. Elouise looked up from the mold and directly at Dune with intensity then, as if seeing her nibbling for the first time. Dune held her auntie's gaze, explanations and mysteries piling up in her throat.

Eventually Elouise spoke. "There are others surviving, gathering data. Different. But I'll have to connect you, these are streams that need to be flowing together."

"What kind of data have they been gathering?"

"Information on the living. Skills. Tracking who's here," Elouise spun her hand around the model. Dune felt disappointed for a moment—data on the living wouldn't help. The disappointment passed, though. She would share what she had. Who knew, maybe new eyes would see the pattern she was missing.

"How have you been living, Dune?" Elouise looked straight at her again. Dune had become quite proficient at foraging in the gardens people had left behind. She was good at shopping in the homes too, but she didn't want to say this to Elouise, it felt dishonest somehow.

"Canning things." She showed Elouise her storage of soups,

stews, jams and sauces. She wanted to impress her auntie, she'd had no one to make proud in quite a while. Elouise had simple questions and they returned to the mundane with ease as they ambled up the stairs to see Mama Vivian.

....

After Elouise left, Dune went back to sit with her grandmother. The song slipped straight from Dune's memory to her throat. Kama had created songs for Dune, her own special songs. Dune knew that she had been held and sung to, and if the memories weren't precise it was ok. These sounds came through and she welcomed them.

Sleep now baby
Baby baby girl
You are the only dream I had
You are the night time hours

Oh sleep now
Hush with all that crying
Mama's got the sweetest kisses
Mama's got the honey baby

Mama Vivian loved lullabies almost as much as she loved gospel.

chapter nineteen

Grin, Grimace

The next morning Dune changed Mama Vivian, rolling up the soiled diaper and gauze cloth she was using to manage her grandmother's scant waste, putting it in a lawn size trash bag she was now keeping in the hall. She had her systems down, she felt no revulsion at her grandmother's papery fragile body, the baby shit and yellow stain. It was all tender life.

She spooned a puree of garlicky lentils and peas into Mama Vivian's mouth, slowly, waiting for the telltale swallow, interspersing the food with sips of water through a bent striped straw.

Mama Vivian accepted this care as if she wasn't really there, not making eye contact with Dune, despondent, not rebellious. She seemed so over it all.

Dune explained that she was going out for a little while, she'd be back by lunchtime. She told her grandmother to stay put, take it easy. This was not a necessary directive, as the old woman no longer seemed interested in getting out of bed, but it comforted

Dune to have said it, casting a protective order over her elder while she was away.

As Dune biked east, over to Elouise's house, she felt like Mama Vivian's detached mood had slipped into her. And with it, her impossible responsibility: every time she left, she risked getting sick far from the old woman, never coming home. Her grandmother relied on her completely now.

She knew there was a selfishness in her persistent work to keep Mama Vivian alive, a stubbornness, a fear of being alone. What value could these empty dying days have for the old woman after such a long and fascinating, powerful, interdependent life?

Dune knew she should let Mama Vivian know it was ok to go, that she didn't have to hold on if she didn't want to. She tried to craft the words in her mind but nothing solidified. The wind moved along her body and the aliveness drifted her mind away from death.

Her grandmother, old and absent but decidedly not sick, without the words of wisdom Dune longed for, was still solace.

It was her first time this far West since Kama was here, weaving through potholes that now had the flavor of sinkholes, wide and mysteriously deep. These portals in the tar told the lie of the paved road, positive proof that there was chaos below. Dune imagined falling into one of the holes and biking straight down, into the salt caves underneath the city, finding the tracks of another underground railroad through the crystalline heaps, coming out into another reality.

Dune had grown up hearing about the massive deposits of salt under this particular earth; her great-grandfather had possibly mined them for a while. As a child hearing these stories, she would ask, "Why isn't the ground white like salt? Is that why vegetables are salty?"

The sun was out and up high, the clouds low and thin. The gray was coming and once it landed it would linger. In Michigan, gray was a season that encompassed most of the fall to spring. When Dune was four, Brendon had taught her that the gray existed in order to make it even better when the sun came out, and she couldn't displace that truth with any adult theories.

She saw two people on her way across McNichols, tucked into their own business. No sick people. It felt almost restful to move through the quiet city, almost like a normal Sunday.

Chippewa Street was mostly grassland now, organized by faint hints of long abandoned lots. Houses had been empty since the 1980s. Some of the houses were officially demolished by the city. The rest was Detroit style ruins, chaotic green mounds of forgotten stone, wood, hearth and yard. Roofs that hung low in the center of an otherwise normal looking building, brick houses with boarded windows, houses with vertical burn lines spilling out the window, heaven bound.

After the water crisis, which Dune had watched from afar in college, tons of garden and farm plots all over the city had been left to wilderness, the bush becoming another way to measure proximity to downtown. Many of the groups that foraged now had learned a lot during the year of water rations—how to harvest what they needed, how to find what could grow on rain water, how lax the fences of community gardens were, upheld more by unspoken boundaries than physical ones.

Big Lou and Elouise's house stood obstinate on the wild block, the yard curated and alive, cared for. There were some wild pheasants in the lot across the street, showing off and calling out to each other. The growing field was reaching toward the pavement. Dune thought she could hear Rouge River.

As she moved towards the bright pink and red wood porch on the white wood building, Dune felt her grandmother's melancholy slipping off of her. Neighbors had complained about Elouise and Big Lou's porch, long ago, called it garish and disruptive. They kept painting it, every summer, outlasting everyone. It looked fresh now.

Dune noticed her anticipation with wry humor; was this her life now? To be excited that someone else would obsess over dying people with her?

The house itself was a bit back from the street and Elouise was sitting on the porch, rocking in her chair, a toothy grin on her face. Dune smiled back, leaning her bike against the front of Elouise's house, deciding not to bother with locking it up. There were more homes, bikes and cars in the city now than there were people, theft wasn't the pressing concern these days. Dune's body came to a stop three steps from the top stair, realizing before her mind did that there was something horribly wrong with Elouise's smile.

"Elouise?"

No answer. Dune tried to move her feet, to run to her aunt and shake her back to this moment, to their plans. But she didn't step forward, she couldn't actually move towards what she was seeing.

Elouise felt larger somehow than she had yesterday. She filled the porch, the yard, the whole street up with her energy. Up close, her face was at war, mouth tilted up in the tight pull of a grimace, eyes grief stricken, seeping, looking into the far distance of the next building. Elouise's hands gripped the arms of the chair, pale with effort, a sign that she'd felt it coming. Her head wrap and top were a golden hue with a green and fuchsia print of leaves and feathers.

Dune wanted to bring her friend a sweater, it was too cold to be out in just the shirt. She stepped closer, wiping sheets of tears from her face. As she stepped onto the porch, she heard the soft whisper-groan from Elouise's mouth, "dih, diiiiiiiiih."

Dune stepped closer, drawn in by the soft breathy sound. Elouise's mouth was moving slowly. Most new grievers, if they had words, spoke them quickly, repeating them, pouring them out.

"Nuuuuuuuuuuuuuuuuuu," exhaled out, a sigh. "Teeeeeeeeee."

Dune shook her head. She wouldn't speak, she knew asking didn't matter. Elouise was sitting here, but now she wasn't.

"Diiiihhh." Breath. "Nuuuuuuuuuuuuuuuuhh." Breath. "Teeeee." Again. And again.

Dune felt close to understanding, on the edge of a foreign tongue.

She was small again, watching *Sesame Street* on Saturday mornings, cereal bowl cupped in her hands to drink the sugary milk that was her highlight of the meal, rapt, egged on by puppets as two pieces of a word she was about to learn crept closer and closer to each other on the tv screen. She wanted the word, whole, on her tongue. When she got it, often before they had figured it out, she would yell it to the foolish puppets. Why couldn't they see it yet?

She squatted down in front of Elouise, looking directly into her friend's absent eyes. She watched Elouise's full lips move ever so slightly around the words. Alive and ghost.

Dignity.

"Dignity." Dune heard it and heard it again, so clearly now.

She turned to see what Elouise's view was from this porch.

Across the street, lot after lot was overrun with wild trees and undergrowth, spilling onto the sidewalk, bursting through an old fence until they were completely contained, intertwined, swallowed by the bush. There was a playground beyond the fence, a slide that descended into ferns, a small tree slipping its branches up between the slats of a wood and chain bridge. There was a recently discarded mattress creeping from the sidewalk into the jungle. The wilderness was not satisfied in the ground, it pushed up through the concrete borders, through the street, long grass, gnarly roots, wild, everywhere. Down the block, two burnt shells of houses. And over the trees, a steeple. Dune tried to remember which church was there.

Just as with Kama, as with everyone she had found, she knew she could not see what they saw. And maybe if she did, it would be the last sight of her life.

Dune touched Elouise's hand and let the grief have her for a long moment. Elouise began to rock faster, just slightly. It was unclear when or why the rocking stopped and started. It happened in all of them, some continued synapse firing off, demanding motion.

When she could stand again, Dune was compelled to find Big Lou. He was either here somewhere and he knew, or he was gone and needed to know.

Or, said the small voice in her head. She ignored it.

She knocked on the front door. Big Lou didn't come.

Cautiously, she stepped inside, a child entering a haunted house on a dare, not wanting to experience whatever was there. Except here the potential terrors were so much worse than plastic skeletons and cottony spider webs.

The kitchen was tiny, cluttered. There was a small pot on the stove with the heat on beneath it. Whatever had been inside the pot had burned to black. Dune turned the flame off. Had Elouise been making her tea?

The table had two plates of breakfast remains, indications of scrambled eggs, the edges of toast. Butter still in its wrapper sat next to one plate, the milk container warming in a puddle of sweat at the center of the table next to a jar of Michigan honey. Dune's body instinctively moved to put the butter and milk in the fridge, gutted, doing this simple thing that Elouise would not do for herself or her husband ever again.

"Lou? Big Lou?"

Her voice moved through the house and brought back nothing. She stepped through the small kitchen to the only door, or rather doorframe, hinges still on one side though the door itself was long gone. Through the door was a short hallway going in both directions.

Directly in front of her on the hallway wall was Elouise's altar to the dead, the foundation of which seemed to consist of wax from a million candles burnt over many years. Dune was moved to see a small picture of Kama laid in front of the hundreds of pictures, funeral programs, beads, bowls of regular water, bottles of Florida water, sticks of sage and incense. In the picture her mother was young, face smirking, hands outstretched like she was telling a crowd to stop applauding. There were oranges and apples on the altar, food for the spirit helpers. There were bundles of chicory root drying, hanging down over the altar. Dune wanted to say a prayer, but could conjure no words. She just touched her fingers over her heart.

To her left were two doors, both open to bedrooms. One room had a messy bed, piles of clothing and shoes at the foot, and a television on with no sound, cheery coppery faced newscasters trying to look serious as captions ran beneath them. Dune stepped in, no Big Lou.

She turned off the television. The bed was mussed in the middle from their sleep.

Grief was an amalgamation of absence narratives, layered over each other. Dune felt her own loss of Elouise and then she felt how Big Lou wouldn't have Elouise to pile up soft next to him anymore.

Dune might never know this feeling, but she longed for it. Perhaps it was worse somehow to know it, to have this kind of old comfortable partnership with routines worn into weighted grooves, sagging steps on the porch, to know this and then not have it. She would never know.

She stepped back and peeked into the other room. Part of Elouise's organizing was around reproductive health and this room was part of the story—it was meant to be a room for a baby, but Elouise's womb had been riddled with painful fibroids and she'd been convinced to have a hysterectomy years ago. Now it was an occasional guest room with an untouched bed, but the star of the room was a crib that had been handed down several generations, lowered and turned into a small desk with piles of old paper stacked on it. The blinds were drawn on the window, as absent of life as the other room was full of it.

He wasn't here, then. Dune returned to the hall, trying to think of where she might find Big Lou, crafting words to give him the news. She didn't want to have the words for this. She stepped forward, past the altar, to the open double door of the living room.

At the threshold of the living room, she gasped. There was Big Lou, on his knees next to the massive picture window that looked onto the front porch of the house. He was facing Elouise's back through the double pane, directly behind her, face buried in his hands, sobbing softly. How had she not heard him? Now the breath of his small sobs seemed amplified. Dune ran over to him and grabbed his shoulders.

"Big Lou, Big Lou I am so sorry!" Dune held him from behind

and cried with him for a while. He didn't notice her, he didn't pause or change in his full body grief. She scrambled back from him then, her shriek loud in the room, realizing that she was alone again.

Fuck, Dune thought. *Take me!*

Her broken heart couldn't take anymore. What was this disease that only seemed to destroy the will to live?

Was it her, did she make people sick? Was it all a punishment for her? What had she done, who had she wronged?

As a child, Dune had learned to apologize before she learned to understand what she had done wrong. Kama's temper was daunting. Dune's only responsibility was to apologize, to say she was sorry, to look sorry, to even be sorry for the mysterious wrong thing she had done. Kama had later apologized for teaching her this and encouraged her to always cultivate her own sense of right and wrong. But now Dune pulled her knees to her chest and yearned to be a child. She wanted to be able to apologize without understanding, to make things right, to leave.

As an adult, there was some right thing to do and not knowing what it actually was—how could she be responsible to her sweet Elouise and to dedicated, caring Lou?

She could call the number the National Guard had posted around, see if they would come. She already knew they couldn't really do anything. Who was going to help them? Who was here for Detroit?

This was the conundrum—to be of a city that didn't want to be saved and didn't want to be abandoned.

Elouise had said the Guard wanted to box her into this death, close up the exits before Big Lou could win his first fight with her. She certainly wouldn't want them to touch her body now.

There was nothing to be done.

How many people were dying like this, quietly slipping away in their own homes?

She couldn't move these two all the way across town with her bike. Even if she got the car, she couldn't do anything for them. The effort of bringing them to her home wouldn't save their lives. It just meant she would get to see every single detail of their deterioration.

Besides, this was their home.

She turned away from Big Lou, slipped out of the dark room, through the hungry kitchen, out onto the porch. Dune took the chair next to Elouise. Before she left, she would get the two of them safe and comfortable inside, perhaps she would lay them next to each other in their bed. She would take pictures of them and place them on her basement wall.

Maybe later she would burn the house down.

But for now, she needed a moment with her auntie. She sat there a long time.

....

Dune went down to the basement and Kama was sitting there next to Elouise, looking at the city. They were talking, soft and low, and didn't notice her approach. Marta was sitting in Brendon's chair over by the washing machine, she wouldn't look up.

Dune walked around the model until she was facing her mother and auntie, only then did they seem to see her. She said something to them, asked them how they were or what they were doing. They looked at each other, twins in motion, and then both started to answer her, but as they spoke, threaded needles appeared near their mouths and pierced, simultaneously, their lower lips. They didn't pause as blood dribbled down their chins, both speaking incomprehensibly, while the needles threaded their mouths closed, right to left. Soon, their lips couldn't move, the thread pulled tight. The women kept making sounds behind their sewn-up mouths and Dune turned to find scissors on the shelf, but. Their mouths were wounds healing smooth. Her search got desperate, emptying the various bins and cups, rifling through drawers.

She woke up still searching.

Before she fell back to sleep, she made a note in her phone. "Cut through silence and lies."

....

Dune's grief came in the form of anger at herself. She had taken so much time for granted. She had wasted hours and hours of quality time with people that she could never see again. So often she had let her mother's words wash over her, not asking questions, not allowing her mother to have honest conversations with her. She had gotten stuck in the prescribed dynamics of any daughter in her teens with a mother who confused love and control. Dune had thought she had time.

It's not that she didn't believe in death, it's that she didn't properly feel it. She didn't understand what happened afterwards, for the people who lived. She'd grown up dabbling on the edge of systemic faith debates that focused on what happened for those who died. They went to heaven, they became nothing, they became everything. Debating that which could not be known didn't matter much to Dune, so she had spent nearly no time worshipping. And she had spent no time exploring the challenge before her now: how was she supposed to survive? And how was she supposed to forgive herself for surviving?

This had been a problem before the syndrome ever came along. She'd had friends get sick, friends in accidents, friends overdose, friends die. Each time, she thought she would have more time with them. She thought they would live forever, or at least the forever of her life. But over and over again, each year since she was 13 years old, someone significant in her life had crossed over, often more than one person.

Some of that was just living in Detroit. It was a hard place to live, it was a hard place to make it through the winter.

Dune had learned, was learning, that when you lose enough people, you stop getting as close to the new ones who come into your life. She stopped looking ahead and started focusing all her attention on the memories. Things used to be so great, so pure, so just, so perfect. We look back and excavate the most beautiful versions of our histories.

Even the blood and gore are more exciting through a generational veil. In real life, death is not very exciting at all. Each time, each time, you see the struggle happening in the body. None of the bodies want to die, all of the bodies are being forced to give up their hold on life through shock or exhaustion. It's not very exciting, when you can't intervene, can't be a superhero come to save the day. We start to realize life gets overwhelmed by death every single time.

But it wasn't only time that Dune had wasted. She'd also forgotten to take seriously just how divergent human minds can be. When she came across those that were different from hers, she tended to get frustrated, trying to change them, trying to make them more positive, solution oriented, easier to be around. Later, she regretted this. She wished that she had seen her mother's genius, and Marta's creativity, Bab's loyalty, Elouise's moral righteousness. She wished she had seen in them all that difference which she could see so clearly now, and let those with the mindsets most challenging to her also be the most exciting.

Dune worked in the basement as much as she could stand it. She had over six hundred profiles now, with growing columns of photos along the wall, watching her. Her project was a solitary collective effort.

The pain of being in the house where her mother had died was too intense sometimes. Dune would risk driving around the wilderness of Detroit streets, winter tires pressing the early snow flat into water. She kept her beams off, using the moon and the light against the snow dusted yards to get around. If she even thought she saw someone she pulled over and tucked down in the car.

But no one else was driving around at night.

chapter twenty

Reality Slips

Marta was laying on the kitchen table, propped up on one elbow. She pushed a spoon towards Dune and then sat up and scooted over, opening her thighs. She lifted her skirt and leaned back on both elbows. Out of her body came what looked like a pale pink ice cream. "Taste it."

Dune picked up the spoon and took the smallest scoop of cream from Marta's pussy. She tasted it—fake strawberry flavor like in frosting or cheap shortcake and maybe rose water?

Dune woke up, sweating as if she'd been having a nightmare. She couldn't quite remember what she'd dreamed about, but knew Marta was in it and that she could feel the pulsing in her body of desire.

She got out of bed and grabbed her cigarette case. She stepped out on the back porch with it and was surprised to see that the moon was full. She could see every single thing. The trees in the yard, mostly stripped of leaves now, were sharp and black against the navy shadow of the night sky.

Across the yard, Dog stood at attention, the moonlight making his coat look silver. She stepped onto the grass, making a small animal sound in her throat to greet him. Dogs were so much easier than humans. Dog sat down, company. She looked back at the shadow she made in the moonlight.

She slipped a joint into her hand and lit it. As she got quiet, she heard the city's night sounds. Something small, skittish, was moving in the yard. There were dogs calling to each other across the city, and she appreciated that Dog didn't feel the need to join in the chorus. As she settled into her high, she sensed something move in the apartment building across the way.

It had been abandoned for some time, the windows mostly broken out with tossed rocks in moments of teenage vandalism. Each year the city threatened to repair it, but nothing changed. Dune was sure that people squatted there in the summer months, though come winter there were better structures. Especially this winter.

And yet she saw something sway in one of the upper windows. And then another. It looked like the moonlight itself, moving against windowpanes that weren't there. Dune watched now, her head tilted back. The movement came again, this time in several windows at once, a swaying. She realized it was a tree, a reflection of a tree, moved by wind.

She slipped back into the house, spooked and goose pimpled, leaning back on the inside of the door. At this angle there is no tree that could be reflected in those windows. There were no windowpanes for a tree to reflect in. There was no wind swaying any of the other trees.

She felt behind her for the lock and turned it.

....

One day, the gardens she knew of were all picked over. Methodically, like an industrial workforce had come and cleared every single piece of fruit, every vegetable, even the weeds, even the rot.

Had the city done this? Was it someone else? Was she angry? Or jealous?

Outside of the emergency relief centers, the streets were generally empty. When she saw other people who were alone and alert, which was now rare, she would wave. Most of these survivor-strangers would scurry away, using isolation as their guard.

If they were open to it, she'd stop and exchange any news and information they were carrying, called across a respectable distance. She asked if they knew where the produce had gone. No one did, they shrugged, or complained with her a bit before moving on. She'd stopped asking other people why they stayed and they'd stopped asking her.

The nature of the sickness had generally lent to flight and depression more than riots and looting. Now it created an energy akin to that of people passing each other in a graveyard, each heading to a separate sadness.

She just wanted some kale. Maybe to invite someone to dinner. She wanted to have an adult conversation.

....

Time no longer correlated to a clock, or to numbers. Time was a dance of light and dark coming in through the windows, lapsed weather patterns, days when the outside world was bearable and days when it wasn't. Time was both binary and a fluid spectrum, including days when she heard news on the radio or didn't, some random measure of when she had energy and when she didn't, a cycle of hunger and fullness.

Now that there were rarely new people to photograph, Dune spent her days piecing together words through the gasps, hitches, repetitions of phrases she'd recorded. She took these fragments and tried to weave them together into a theory of what was happening to her city, moving with her hands extended into a forever fog.

When she finally ran out of steam, Dune slept in Kama's room, the bag of bones on her mother's side, a boundary that had held even after her father's death. She now slept in her father's spot. No matter when she went to sleep, she woke up with the light, laying there in peace for a few minutes, until the present moment fully returned to her.

She hadn't been a coffee drinker before H-8, but now she liked all the Alice in Wonderland feelings she could produce, injecting emotions into the numb cycle of her life. She would pour herself a cup and give herself ten seconds to miss real liquid milk from a cow. There was none left in the city—the distributed stuff was powder.

Such regrets were part of her cycle.

Coffee, breakfast. Vivian care, clean up.

Then back to the basement, seeking, listening and seeking.

chapter twenty-one

Vivian Waits to Die

Vivian wasn't sick. She was old, mostly deaf, tired of being alive, grieving her daughter-in-law, and her son, and her husbands, her friends. This wasn't supposed to be her final scene, outliving everyone.

She was experiencing the underwhelming privilege of a slow, normal death in the midst of a pandemic. She didn't feel curious anymore, she'd seen the cycle over and over: greed, war, victimhood, demands. Vivian felt sure that whatever was happening, humans had caused it with a million selfish decisions. It was the anthropocene. She knew evolution was possible, but she didn't have anything left to give towards it.

Every time Dune left, Vivian half hoped the girl would make a run for it. To Greece, to Vietnam, south. She wanted to tell the child this, but nothing happened when she thought the words, trying to push them through the habit of her silence, which by now had its own persistent, pathetic weight.

She didn't have the strength anymore to even change herself.

If the girl ghosted like Kama and Bab, Vivian knew she would die in her own shit. She was glad her Wes hadn't lived to see her like this. He'd died while she was still strong, capable. His last words to her had been, "I am ready, just cain't turn from yo tireless beauty."

This ... he wouldn't recognize her. She had seen and loved him in his own deteriorated state, but didn't think men could move through the repellant phases of life so easily, they were still shielded from so much of the making. She was grateful he was spared her undignified demise. *Not very feminist in my old age*, she thought, with humor.

Even now, she was waiting for the humiliation of her granddaughter's help. Again. The wet was cooling beneath her. She had fallen down a month ago, maybe longer, time was confusing. Her body was stiffening daily into a bone cage. Only movement kept a body supple. She prayed that she was too old to recover.

But she hadn't died yet.

Until very recently she had been walking around and feeling pretty good about herself, able to leverage her body using upper arm strength against a cane, balancing her three-legged operation around the house and maintaining a sliver of independence. She still had all her marbles upstairs. She'd stood up, watched Dune cremate Kama, heard the private, involuntary sounds of grief loud enough to reach her naked ears.

But she'd fallen again after that, a silly fall from moving too fast. She'd gotten herself up before Dune could catch her flailing on the floor, pulled herself up the stairs to her room. Vivian hadn't been able to lift herself much since then and didn't even want to.

There were things she had never said to Kama, had been saving for her death bed. She cursed this failed plan daily. Had she not learned that lesson with Brendon, his body destroyed while she had apologies on her tongue? Now she had to lay in bed with her regrets and let the child wipe and feed her.

Not child. Dune was aging quickly as Vivian watched.

Some days ago, Dune had come home distraught. Someone else was gone, but Vivian couldn't guess who. Dune had stopped in and said hello with a raw face, and then disappeared down to the basement. The girl seemed better when she came back up, as if she had put something together, or away, or in order. She'd always had that way about her, seeking order and satisfied by it.

Vivian didn't mind order, but she was a deconstructionist at heart. She couldn't deconstruct this moment, pull it into neat pieces in her mind and find the part that was wrong, out of sync. Her mind was not working quite right anymore. Now she needed someone who had come out of her own body, once removed, to wipe her like a baby.

It made her furious. Most of the time she just waited to die, not thinking about something beyond, about reuniting with loved ones like Wes had promised, or reincarnating like her parents had believed.

She just wanted to end this current experience.

Everyone around Vivian was dying, had died. The whole city was dying—young, old, friend, foe. It had been dying for decades, in a variety of ways: economic, cultural, visceral. She'd believe that capitalism would die and then the people would truly be able to survive. She never imagined the people going first.

Places can be so confusing in their death throes, convinced that longevity lends permanence, history yields opportunity—that because a city was built, it has a right to exist. That if it ceased, it failed.

Vivian knew some Detroit would exist for someone, she hoped for Black people. She was more interested in communities than in the structure of a city, or a nation. But after years of fierce battles for the future of this place, she didn't think the people she counted as her own, as loved ones, would make it to that future Detroit, where their lives were not pure struggle. She had believed in the necessity of struggle when everyone was still alive. Struggle with this much misery was too heavy. She wanted everyone still here to simply find a place that felt like home, and felt free.

This home, where she could feel Brendon and the foolish amazing Kama, this was where she wanted to cross over. But, somehow, she couldn't get free of this ancient body.

She didn't want to go on like this, unable to muster the care with which to communicate, losing every capacity, dependent on another for everything. Everyone else was getting something, some disease that manifested by freezing people in what looked like the first private shock of grief, making it impossible to function. This she had slowly pieced together from seeing Kama, Bab, watching Dune.

She didn't think she would get this disease. She had watched her loved ones die from cancer, AIDS, diabetes, heart attack, stroke, flu, polio, leprosy, sickle cell anemia, time, stress, violence, addiction, war, accidents and heartbreak. Even grief. Everything had come and swept through her friends, her husbands, her comrades, her child. And she was still here.

She'd known so much grief, perhaps by now she was immune.

Dune had fashioned a knocker in the hallway, with a cord to Vivian's bed, but Vivian had dropped the end of it while napping and couldn't tell if it was in the sheets somewhere, or on the floor. She felt so fucking helpless. She thought, again, *dying is a bitch*.[4]

"Dune!" she yelled, perhaps. Vivian heard nothing.

Raising Brendon, she had never really considered that her only child might die before she did. Brendon, hit by a bus. Dead immediately, if the body held on a few hours. He was standing on a street corner, so random, he rarely even walked anywhere. And then he was hit and gone. Such devastating incompletion.

After that, Vivian just hadn't had anything to say, nothing that mattered enough to open her mouth for it. Then it just became more comfortable than trying to engage in meaningful conversations about anything other than Brendon. Now, she wished she could offer Dune the solace of her voice, but couldn't tell if she still had one.

She gathered volume up through her body from the soles of her gnarled feet to get her voice to the door. She couldn't hear herself, but she felt the movement of sound in her chest. Was she that deaf? She had no idea if anything was coming out of her mouth.

It had been twenty whole years since she'd watched her beloved Wes die, caring for his cancerous body until he left it. His prostate had betrayed him.

She'd met him when she was a brilliant forty-one year-old, in Detroit to study movement for a year. They'd both been married to others when their intellectual and political partnership had become a primary relationship in their lives. They'd realized that there was a safety in the realm of politics and philosophy that could help them survive scandal and the traumas of the heart.

One time, at the beginning of their friendship, they shared early life histories of trauma that neither of them particularly wanted to revisit. They never spoke of those things again—for forty years those histories lived on in silence and in the deep mutual respect they had for each other as people who didn't use their trauma to succeed in life. They had survived and they had loved others, and both had children, and now they had found each other for a second long chapter of life. Their passion kept them in the realm of debate and conversation and movement.

Life.

Even now, she still turned to him in her mind, wanting to tell him unfolding theories, to hear his thoughts on this latest crisis.

She hadn't expected to go too far beyond Wes in this life. But here she had lived a whole other life, experienced the need for her political voice in the city—there were so many conversations, there was so much to learn and teach. She had developed routines for her health and thinking. Then she'd written her own articles, given her own speeches, articulated her own political vision for and from this city. She'd learned to argue with people in ways that strengthened them, made them stand up for their ideas. And then, when her words left, she'd listened.

She'd experienced the exquisite grief of losing her only child. She had cried quiet, private tears. And now she was in this little room at the back of her dead son's house with moments of Dune for company, silent, or singing. Or the radio at full blast next to her, giving her pre-digested snippets of news. Her mind was almost empty of thoughts.

Her granddaughter was one of these girls who dressed like a boy and dated other girls, which had never bothered Vivian. Dune was a glowing golden brown that went sallow in winter and she often wore her hair in soft braids down her back. That, and Brendon's delicate features tipped slightly rounder by Kama's blood, made her look like a perpetual teenager.

She was gaining weight as Mama Vivian watched, fairly quickly.

Vivian had seen this before and understood it. Dune was making a mother for herself out of her own body, her massive grief.

Vivian had loved guiding the young girl into the realms of philosophy and theory, sharing her grandchild's life questions and struggles, talking about concepts of self-transformation. Vivian found it fascinating how soon children were selves. Dune had been so bright of mind from the beginning.

She wanted to comfort Dune, but she had forgotten how.

Since the plague started, Dune had kept Vivian company as best she could, trying to tell Vivian about the outside world, yelling words that longed to be whispered. Closed captioned news had helped her come to terms with the likelihood that Kama and Bab were victims of a plague, were gone-gone. Vivian watched Dune struggle with the language, the emotions that came with trying to explain that the world was ending, here, all around them.

Ultimately, she knew most of what was happening by the look on the child's face.

Vivian gathered her volume again and cried out, "Dune!" feeling silent in spite of all the effort. She did experience a short fit of coughing that grabbed her whole chest. That would surely be heard, she thought. She closed her eyes.

She felt Dune's hands on her before she was aware the girl was in the room. One small firm hand on Vivian's chest, the other slipping behind her back. It calmed Vivian down to be held this way, as if her heart itself was being cupped and soothed.

Vivian looked up and saw Dune's mouth moving, heard the muted sound of a voice, tried to hear the child across the small gap between them. Nothing. She shook her head to let Dune know nothing was coming through. The child smiled, though there was still a deep sadness in her eyes.

"I—sorry! I went—more food!" Dune spoke loud, close to Vivian's left and slightly better ear.

Vivian nodded. She didn't care much for food these days. Her best days were softened by vodka.

Now, floating in the girl's palms, she remembered that she needed to be changed. She hadn't gotten used to the idea of asking Dune for that help, pointing to herself in the way the child had asked her to.

She'd had a small stroke four years before and her care at home had been a trio of professional women, strong through the shoulders, who came walking in with gloves on and changed her swiftly, nonchalantly, while yelling their hellos. She hadn't seen them in a long time.

Dune, who was small-boned, had a slower, steadier way about her. She required Vivian to work, grasping the railing to hold her upper body up, pressing her heels down into the soft bed to lift her own hips. It was exhausting.

A slight shift of Dune's nose let Vivian know the girl was aware of the need. Vivian was embarrassed. She'd always smelled like jasmine flower and lilac, and her lovers had told her they missed her smell when she was away from them. Now Dune pulled back Vivian's sheet and together they began the slow ritual of rolling and scooting and pulling and wiping, the shit, shit, shit that now marked the hours of Vivian's life.

When Vivian was once again dry and arranged against her pillows, Dune brought the straw of the water glass to her lips. Vivian loved the feeling of cool clear water over her tongue. She needed to figure out how to ask the girl to get her some more vodka and orange juice, though. That would make this all a little easier.

She was looking up at her granddaughter trying to figure out how to get a stiff drink when she saw Brendon enter Dune's face, right there, his beautiful face embedded in her features.

She knew Dune looked like her father, but this was different, this was Brendon. He was looking at her with total adoration, like he had as a child, before losing his father, before their parallel lives in the Black power struggle, before he felt abandoned by her lack of enthusiasm for Kama.

Her womb, surely no more than a raisin now, swelled and started deep inside her, remembering the feeling of his life forming inside her body, knowing that he was gone, that this innocent loving look was gone.

His face didn't waver. She knew then that she was dying and she felt herself fill all the way up with gratitude. She moved her hand on top of Dune's and giggled at Brendon's face. It wasn't her whole life flashing in front of her, it was the grace of her life, solid as flesh.

....

Her grandmother slipped away between Dune's hands.

Dune didn't know what made Mama Vivian look at her with such wonder, glee. Her grandmother passed on from life with her eyes open, unfocused. Dune felt gratitude in her bitterness, that her last family member managed to die peacefully, not contorted with pain.

Dune held on for hours, remembering. She let the night come and go, there by her grandmother's side.

When the light was up the next morning, Dune slipped a rug under the chair by her grandmother's bed and moved the body into it, sliding it down the hall. Getting down the stairs was the most challenging part, leaning her back against the wall and holding Mama Vivian up with her arms across her grandmother's chest as if they were in the ocean, drowning.

She could feel the difference between this body and her mother's—Mama Vivian seemed to have light bird bones in her old skin. When she finally got to the backyard, she placed the body into the same shallow fire pit where she had burned Kama, and then Red, out of this world. She used the last of the dry wood to get the fire going, as well as two old chairs and a table Brendon had started.

Dune went inside, upstairs to Vivian's bookshelves. She pulled down Hegel, Marx, Plato, Herodotus, Mao, Castro, Malcolm, Baldwin and two of the twenty signed copies of Wes's autobiography. She thought it fitting that Vivian should disappear in a flame of her favorite words. As the books transformed the fire into high reaching flames and the sheet started to burn, Dune looked away, overcome with longing.

"If I get sick out here, right now, I could fall into the fire and die really fast, before I soil myself. Maybe I could just throw myself on the fire." She wondered if her soul would blend with Mama Vivian's if she hopped on now, like death was a magic carpet ride and she just needed to figure out a way to climb on it and go.

Where did they do that, the wives throwing themselves on the burning bodies of deceased husbands, the expectation of sacrifice as a final duty? Images of fire and rivers far away flanked by monks in red robes flitted through her mind. She felt deep respect.

Detroit was far away too. Poverty and oppression always distanced itself in the US, like it had been brought from somewhere else, could only be compared to somewhere else, somewhere Third. But this was how the American experiment started, this was all it ever was. Dune's thinking cut a rough smile over her face, feeling comfort in this Vivian type of thought: dialectical humanism, the reverb of capitalism, the boomerang of smallpox.

Dune peeked at the fire before her, and saw a black wetness that turned her stomach before she looked back to the sky. Dune had watched every moment of her mother's cremation, the way the skin had undone itself in the heat. She'd inhaled the strange smells of hair and skin becoming sky.

She never needed that experience again. Once the fire sounded solid and internal, she stepped back, looking everywhere else.

"Don't leave me," she thought then, unsure to who. Then she begged aloud, to everyone who was long gone, "Don't leave me."

She stepped further back and then went inside the house, moving from one undoable task to another.

When she'd returned to add broken chair legs to the fire half an hour later, it had been popping with muscles and fat. Tomorrow, amongst the coals, there would be bones. Once they cooled, she would recover what she could and create an altar of bones in Mama Vivian's room.

She couldn't get warm in the empty house. She went to the basement, bringing Mama Vivian's afghan from the living room for her lap. She held her elbows and rested her head on the edge of the model of Detroit. The syndrome was everywhere, as slow and persistent as the green mold growing outwards all around her model house.

She cried on and off, raining on the edge of the city, a little pool. She didn't tell her father that his mother was dead. It felt too obvious.

"Perhaps I should burn this too," she thought. Perhaps to rise from its own ashes, Detroit needed a cleansing fire ritual. She didn't quite sleep, but she dreamt.

....

Dune was walking down the middle of the street. It had rained, it was gray everywhere, but she could see rainbows in each of the puddles. Her house was a few blocks down and her family was in front, Kama, Brendon and Vivian, playing a game where they were chasing each other. Playing. She wanted to play. She felt her child-self opening up in her system.

Dune started to run towards them and jumped in the first puddle, felt it splash up around her. The world was gray but the water had a million colors in it. She ran and splashed through the next puddle, and then ran and jumped up even higher and smashed down into the next puddle—but the puddle had no bottom and she was inside it, falling through the bright water, falling so deeply.

She tried to kick upwards, push with her hands back up to the surface, she hadn't taken a breath. There was light, and she swam towards it, coming up just as she was about to explode for need of air. She pulled herself up on the edge of the puddle, but now she wasn't on her street anymore. The water was salty on her lips and this world looked utterly bright. She pulled herself up, out of the water, onto her knees, and then up to standing.

All she could see in every direction was flat sand, the sun beating down on her. Looking down, she realized the puddle was vaporizing in the heat, already too small for her to fit through. She dropped down and put her hands in the water, as the puddle disappeared.

Then she sat back on the sand, shocked. She held up her neat smooth wrists, both of her hands gone to the other side. She sat still, trying to think. But thinking made her cry, and she cried and cried until, looking down, the puddle was returning. She cried until the puddle was wide, until she could see rainbows in it. Then she dove in.

....

The next night she couldn't sleep. Again.

It wasn't for lack of exhaustion. She was so weary it seized up in the center of her back and dried out her eyes.

It was all the absence. There was nothing she needed to do. There was nothing interesting for her to watch, nothing she wanted to read or listen to. There were just these hours, long dark hours where her dreams worried her sleep and the truth worried her waking.

There were things she didn't want to discuss: The strange snippets of dreams she could remember. All the ways she wasn't Kama, or Mama Vivian. Marta, who appeared in her dreams, generally to disappear again. The mold growing all over random spots on her model of Detroit. The death growing all over the city within and beyond her doors.

She let the night become her company. In the darkness she spoke, to herself, to Mama Vivian, to Kama, to Brendon. She told her secret and mundane thoughts.

She tried to feel that she was alive, but she wasn't sure, not sure enough.

At 3 AM, her songs would sometimes show up.

She missed singing for Mama Vivian. Over the last few months, getting to sing for her grandmother, they had had some of the sweetest, most intimate moments of their long relationship. Not in conversation, not in debate and training, not in analysis. Just singing, being quiet, and singing some more. The sweet reception on Vivian's face, the pure love.

With this on her heart, she let the songs come, almost always humming first, and then letting the words flow in. They came in the dark, in the living room where she had gotten in the habit of ending her nights with a spliff, more weed in the balance each night.

When she smoked, she sang the cigarette song.

Coming in, coming in
Toxic things and poison
Going out, going out
Freedom once again

chapter twenty-two

Alone

Dune lay on the couch in the living room under a blanket.

The vines between the houses were dazzling burnt orange. Earlier that day a hawk had landed up in the tree, near the top of the window, a smaller bird clutched in his talons. As Dune had watched, he had plucked the smaller bird clean and eaten all he could from its small carcass. He'd dropped it when he took off. Dune could still see some of the feathers caught in the bright vines. Change in the natural world was so beautiful, so inevitable. Why didn't it feel like that, to be human?

The leaf got to be brilliant before it let go. Kama got no chance, Mama Vivian faded away.

Dune had eaten and there was nothing she needed to do, no one to care for, no one to call for her, no one to ignore her. She felt guilt as soon as she realized what she was feeling, before she let it crystalize into a thought. Her guilt wasn't large enough to quiet the thought.

She was grateful to be alone finally, truly alone. She knew, in her bones that she was going to have to find people if she was going to survive. She knew that there were people, somewhere, people like her parents, like Mama Vivian, people who were making a way out of no way. And she would have to find them, and beg them to let her in, and find a way to let them in. She knew that.

But first she needed this curling in, this bright release of all the lives she'd loved and lost.

....

The next time Dune went to the basement, there were trees on the model.

Specifically, there was a leaf on a stem growing up from the gray lego plastic of her model yard. Another in the northeast corner of the model, which some small voice in her head noted was near Elouise's street. And down by the river, new leaves.

They looked like trees, scaled against the small roads and game houses. They weren't toys, weren't plastic—they had sprung up there on their own.

Dune touched the leaftree a few blocks from Elouise's home, down to where it sunk into the foam board. She squatted down on resistant knees and looked under the table. There were a few tiny tendrils, slender green hairs curling down from the pocked belly of the table, one almost to the vase below.

She had been keeping the heat down in the house, in case that was inviting the mold that kept creeping onto her model. But it didn't seem to matter. Dune looked around the basement again, for sun, water, seeds, gardeners. Shadows. Ghosts. Anything to explain this little life.

There was no explaining it. She thought the word magic and immediately felt a chill. She had tried wiping the mold off the model to no avail. She didn't even try to pull this green out. It didn't seem like weeds.

....

Three days later, leaning against a building in the dusk, Dune tried to catch her breath.

Two blocks behind her was an evacuation paddy wagon. She'd been out walking around in the first hard snow of the season, letting the flakes touch her face. Coming around the corner from Mack to Second she'd spotted a white van ahead, with two soldiers dragging a third person, resisting.

Dune had immediately slipped back, leaning against the brightly graffitied wall of the small abandoned building that dominated this corner. Then she had run, zig zagging snowy blocks until she had come around to Alexandrine and Second. Her body seemed to need twice the oxygen she could inhale and she worried that everyone in a three-block radius could hear her wheezing.

She peeked around the corner, through a thicket of evergreen bushes coated in snow. The van was now rolling slowly in her direction.

She stumbled back from the corner and ducked into an alley. Hearing the van, Dune dropped to her stomach, the cold air buffeting in the snow and dew-dropping her upper lip. Would they see her bright breath?

She scooted forward and looked out of the alley. The van drove down Second slowly, the soldiers in the front seat with gas masks and guns pointing out the front windows. The van passed from her view.

Dune waited until she couldn't hear the engine any longer, and then a long time after that, until the cold had penetrated her layers and her fingers started to feel numb. Slowly she walked onto Second, looking in both directions up and down the wide road to be sure the van was out of sight. She pulled off a glove and used it to erase her footsteps, in case anyone got interested in following her through the snow. She walk-jogged back down her street, doubling around to enter off the back alley.

....

It wasn't her birthday, not until March. There was no reason for a cake, no need for it. Especially not a cake made from powder in a box, best paired with frosting from a plastic container.

Still, when she'd seen the Moist Strawberry Supreme cake box all alone on the baking aisle shelf, she'd added it to the cart full of canned tuna, sardines and anchovies, polenta and frozen crab cakes. She'd sought out chocolate and found some unsweetened super dark bars which she planned to combine with sugar and pray into a frosting. All of this in abundance, she rolled past the un-humaned cashier lanes and loaded her car. That would be her last time at University Market because there was nothing left that anyone should be eating now and the paper products were gone.

She drove home thinking only of the cake, while also sort of thinking of nothing, veering slow around potholes, her car lights off in the darkness. It was the first single digit cold snap of the year and the city was white, icy.

She parked a few blocks away from home, just in case. She unloaded the groceries she'd found, moving slowly, her attention extended around her in a 360. Foraging season was over. She had enough food, water, supplies. She didn't need to go anywhere, not for a while.

Kama had kept a spare key to several of the neighbors' homes and Dune had decided to use the Thorn's kitchen as a winter pantry. They could work it out later. Dog found her in her unloading process, and followed her as she ran two bags at a time a few steps, setting them down and going back for the other two, doubling the distance and then repeating the process. Dog knew it wasn't a game and stood watch over whichever bags she left behind.

Once she got to her own door with just the bag full of the cake items, she looked back at Dog for a long minute. She had never been interested in animals inside a house. She thought it was gross on the part of the humans and cruel to most of the animals.

But it was cold as fuck out there.

She held the door open and made a face at Dog that she hoped was both inviting and held a standard around potty training. Dog was cautious, stepping inside the door. He crossed the threshold of the kitchen and sat down, looking up at her as she unloaded her groceries. Once she finished, he took a few steps down the hall and looked back at her. She followed him. He kept going until he reached the bathroom. Inside, he walked over to the bathtub, pawing at its porcelain edge.

Dune laughed. "Bet."

She gave Dog a warm soapy bath. He smelled like it had been a long time. He kept trying to drink the water from the faucet.

"You can come spend time here. But you don't have to stay. You can. But you don't owe me anything, ok? Just knock on the door when you want to go out."

When she finished rinsing him off, Dog stood very still and looked at her, then at the shower curtain, and back at her. She pulled the curtain and he shook himself off for several minutes. When she opened the shower curtain, it was with some trepidation.

"Smart dog."

Dog jumped out of the tub and dove into the towels she had lined the floor with, over and over again, pressing his ears and neck down into the fluff. He seemed like a normal golden retriever mutt, young, playful.

Damp Dog followed Dune through her house. She pulled out the cake box. One egg, ⅓ cup oil, 1 cup water, cake mix, 350 degrees for thirty-five minutes. Dune swapped in apple sauce as an egg substitute. She sat at the table while it cooked. Then she stood up and found a few leftover chicken thighs in the fridge and cut them up for Dog. He ate quickly and she felt good to help him in this way.

When she pulled the cake out and tested it with a fork, she could feel in her gut the anticipation. She opened a book of poems by Tongo Eisen-Martin that Kama had celebrated as revolutionary, and she read out loud to Dog while her cake cooled. She only distorted the surface a few times in the frosting process.

She didn't look for candles because that would have been a lie. She was an adult with no one to lie to. She saw Dog watching her. "I celebrate your move-in day." She cut herself one piece and ate it.

It was good.

Endnotes

1.   Grace Lee Boggs was an American revolutionary who dedicated her life to studying and organizing for liberation.

2.   Original quote from Jimmy Boggs, Detroit labor organizer and philosopher.

3.   This line is borrowed from Detroit Activist Mama Sandra Simmons of Hush House.

4.   This was spoken by Grace Lee Boggs during her time in hospice.

Acknowledgments

I want to thank my parents Jane and Jerry Brown, who never balked when I declared myself a writer. Mom thank you for the gentle laughter and "of course" every time I remembered I needed to write fiction. Thank you to my sisters April and Autumn, both gifted writers, who have flanked me such that I could find and be myself. Thank you Detroit, especially the Black liberation and food justice movements, especially the Allied Media Projects crew, for showing me how we envision a post-capitalist future. Thank you Ill Weaver and Jenny Lee and Detroit Summer for bringing me to Detroit. Thank you Grace Lee Boggs, Charity Hicks, David Blair, Sheddy and my other Detroit ancestors for the love and lessons. Thank you Tananarive Due, the inaugural VONA Speculative Fiction Class and the Clarion Writers Workshop for giving feedback on early versions of this work. Thank you Janine de Novais, Dani McClain, Jodie Tonita, Sofia Santana, Shane Jones, my goddesses and inner circle for repeatedly affirming my fiction heart. Thank you Sage Crump and Mia Herndon for letting me be me and still belong. Thank you Sofia, Bernie Cox, Evan Mallon, Bobby Bermea, and Tchaiko Omawale for deep reading and feedback and continuing to ask me about the work. Alexis de Veaux thank you deeply for the feedback I needed to finish. Thank you AK Press for years of positive writing experiences and for connecting me with Black Dawn, and thank you Sanina Clark for trusting that this could be the launch of the imprint, for saying the magic words "novella trilogy." And finally, thank you to my fiancé Nalo Zidan for the big romance that creates a soft place for moving all this grief through.